MONROSE LEGACY

Sarah's Inheritance

BOOK 1

J. D. PLACE

To order additional copies of this book, contact:
Xlibris Corporation
1-888-795-4274
www.Xlibris.com
Orders@Xlibris.com
41768

For O. Walter Place

I give a great big thanks to my friend, Quin Lemons, who read and proof the many drafts of the book and listen untirelessly to my ramblings about the plot and characters. Thank you, Quin, for your encouragement and enthusiasm.

Preface

The story in this book takes place in August 1992. The U.S. economy is starting to move into recession. Airplane travel does not require one to take their shoes off going through security or lining up at security gates before passing through the ticket line. Times are a little simpler; air travel is not as much a hassle as today—Homeland Security does not exist yet.

In August 1992, a family in Massachusetts goes through changes they never thought possible. One document turns their world upside down. One family member betrays their relatives in pursuit of riches, while another wrestles with a change in career direction and a revelation that changes how she views herself in the family.

Chapter 1

"That's not the deal, Henry. That's not the deal. Payment is not due for thirty days. Why are you calling for the payment in two weeks?" Elliot almost shouted into the phone. He was trying to maintain his composure. After listening for a moment, he said, "No, don't do that. It's just that I have no capital available right now. And I won't have the money for the payment until a week before it's due." Beads of perspiration started trickling down his face as he listened again. "I'll see what I can do to get part of the payment to you by then. *What? Thursday, next week?*"

Elliot slammed the phone down. Henry wanted the entire payment in two weeks. If it were a smaller sum, he could do what he'd always done when Henry did this. *Where I am going to get all of that money? I could do a part of it that way. And the rest?*

He should have sold Star Dust Textiles when he had the opportunity. But Uncle Bill and the board vetoed the sale. He was now sure he could have gotten around Uncle Bill and convinced enough of the board members to approve the sale. Then he wouldn't have been in such a tight fix for cash right now. He and his uncle rarely ever saw eye to eye on how to run the business. His uncle had told him on several different occasions that he didn't keep enough cash ready to cover emergencies. Uncle Bill hadn't liked the way Elliot played everything close to the wire as Elliot kept some of the business deals from his uncle and the board. "It's going to bring the business down around our ears if you keep doing what you're doing," his uncle would say.

As soon as I pay off Henry, I'll be free of him, Elliot thought. He wouldn't play at any of his casinos again. Now that he had control of the Monrose funds, he could build his own casinos. Monroe Industries would be the front. No one knew he had set up a Swiss bank account where each month a little of the corporation's money found its way. *I have plans, dear Uncle Bill, and you are not here to interfere,* he thought, grinning. The family was quick to agree to the cremation; Elliot mused as he gazed out the window, watching a plane disappear into a cloud as it took off from Boston's Logan Airport.

Elliot knew where he could get part of the money. He would be all right as long as the accountants didn't audit the books. According to the latest memo, no audit was due in two months. If everything went as it should, the money would not be missed. When Elliot took over Monrose Industries, he put a stop to the finance account security system his uncle had installed before he died, explaining to the company's Information Systems Department there were some bugs that needed to be worked out by the software company.

Elliot's intercom buzzed. He pushed the button, and his secretary's voice announced, "Mr. Rhodes is here for his two o'clock appointment."

"Send him in," Elliot responded. He wished he had the rest of the afternoon free.

Elliot put on his jacket, half wishing he didn't have this dinner engagement with the representative from Hanover Trust, but it might work to his advantage since the employees would see him leave for the evening. On his way out, he left a few instructions regarding meeting arrangements for his secretary to take care of in the morning.

Driving home afterward, Elliot thought the evening went well with the Hanover representative. *There were some possibilities there.* At his condo overlooking Boston Gardens, Elliot changed clothes, checked his messages, then called Elaine.

It was after 11:00 p.m. when Elliot reached the office tower. Parking his black BMW sedan in the next block, Elliot made his way with caution to the building. Lights in the buildings around him indicated some people were still working. He didn't want to be seen. A guard was in the front lobby. *That was good.* He sneaked around to the parking lot side of the building and went in at the entrance. Elliot knew the alarm on the side door would not be armed for another fifteen minutes. He studied the activities of those working in the building, especially their arrivals and departures. It gave Elliot a sense of power to know where everyone was for times like this.

Making his way with feline stealth to his office, Elliot turned on the lamp at his desk and sat down in front of his computer. He turned it on, keyed in the password, and started the process of transferring funds.

Chapter 2

"Sarah, Sarah!" She looked around and saw Mrs. Greyson coming down the walk, waving to her. Sarah waited beside her brown Toyota Corolla. "It's so good to see you. It's such a beautiful Sunday. Had a good sermon this morning?"

"Yes, we had a guest minister from Knoxville. He spoke on a timely topic—drugs and their effect on society," replied Sarah.

"It seems that's one of the biggest problems of these times. It's a shame so many people think it's the 'in' thing, or that they can use drugs to escape from their problems. If only they would turn to God. We both know God takes care of his children's challenges."

"I certainly do," replied Sarah, thinking of how well God was taking care of her needs.

"We had a good turnout in church and Sunday school. Mrs. Webb wasn't feeling well this morning, so I taught her class," Mrs. Greyson continued.

"Do you have your car with you, or do you need a ride home?"

"I left my car at my grandson's. He and his wife live around the corner. They've asked me to join them for lunch and tell them a few stories about the old homeplace. Would you like to join us?"

"Thank you, but I want to work on the oral history interview I did with Adie. I need to have it completed for our September Historical Society meeting."

"Oh, she is a charming person. I hope I'm as spry as she is when I'm her age. She has certainly seen and done a lot. Anytime you want to see the old homeplace, give me a call. Veny and his wife would love to show it off. Don't forget the oral history meeting tomorrow night. Enjoy your day," she said. Mrs. Greyson smiled as she turned and hurried down the street.

"Thank you. And I will," Sarah called after her.

Sarah unlocked the Corolla's door and got in. She was grateful to count Mrs. Greyson as a new friend, also a resident of Thoroughbred Acres where Sarah was living now. She showed Sarah around Roswell and introduced her to a few people residing in her building. Mrs. Greyson pointed to her the direction of the grocery stores and post offices, and together they explored the linen and antique shops. Sarah also learned from Mrs. Greyson that her grandson worked for the local police department. When her grandson married five years ago, she gave the family home to him and his bride as a wedding present and moved to Thoroughbred Acres.

———————

It certainly is a nice day, Sarah thought. *I'll go over to Vickery Creek at the old Roswell mill for lunch. One thing about this area—every day is a beautiful day.*

The gentle breeze caressed Sarah as she sat on the porch of the mill. She quickly laid her fork on the napkin to keep it from blowing off the table. She enjoyed the sound of the rushing water from the creek below and the mass of green leaves dancing on the hillside as she waited for her order to be served. This was one of the places she had put on her list to share with Jason.

She had read about the old mill last year in a historical novel. The mill was burned during the Civil War by Union soldiers, with the workers arrested and sent to the northern prisons for manufacturing wool for Confederate uniforms, considered an act of treason. Sarah, moved by the story, had wanted to visit the place ever since. She wondered what happened to the mill workers—mostly women and children—wondered if any of them found their way back here.

A believer in historic preservation, Sarah was delighted to discover the mill was renovated into an indoor mall. The exterior was restored, including the waterwheel, while shops, restaurants, an art gallery, and photographer's studio claimed the interior floors of the two-story mill.

A large hole in the wooden floor of the front upstairs hall surrounded by a handrail allowed visitors to look downstairs on a model train display. The small trains went through tunnels and past a tiny replica of the Roswell train station and a small version of the town of Roswell in days of long ago. Sarah was among the adults and children who delighted in watching the train move along the tracks.

I certainly want to share this place with Jason. I guess he's probably eating lunch too. It had been four and a half weeks since she last saw hubby Jason waving to her as she backed the Corolla out of the driveway. If she hadn't been laid off, they would still be together in Salem. She missed him. *Maybe I should take a break from job hunting and visit him. Surprise him?* That sounded like fun.

The events of the past four months had almost overwhelmed her. Why do changes seem to occur in bunches? The recent changes in her life had started with Uncle Bill's death, followed by her being laid off two weeks later, and then leaving Jason and Salem. Losing her job was the catalyst that prompted them to move. They had vacationed here frequently over the past five years, enjoying the warm weather and the many things to see and do. For the past three years, they had talked about moving to Atlanta—now they were here. It was hard leaving Jason. He had stayed in Boston to finish several projects for the company, which would take no more than three months. Then he'd move down here to start a branch office. He had encouraged her to come here to get a head start on finding a job and look for a house to buy.

Sarah was surprised when Uncle Bill left her some money, although they had always been close. They had a good time when she worked at the company during the summers of her college years. She had a lot of good memories of Uncle Bill. Her thoughts were interrupted by the waiter's setting her food on the table.

Sarah turned off the main road onto the drive that leads to the apartment complex where she lived—Thoroughbred Acres.

She had learned through the leasing agent that the land on which the complex was built was once a horse farm. The building now used as a recreation center was at one time an actual stable, which housed about twenty thoroughbred horses. The farm had over three hundred acres in its prime. The agent said about one hundred acres was forest. Not much was left of the forest now. The creek that had once watered thoroughbreds flowed under the bridge into a pond ahead, glimmering in the sun. The willows along the end of the pond were blown by a gentle breeze.

One of these afternoons, I'm going to take a blanket and a book and sit along the pond's edge and read, Sarah thought to herself.

What impressed Sarah about all the apartment complexes she had visited while looking for a place to live was the gorgeous landscaping. Entrances to the apartment complexes contained begonias, impatience, petunias, and other summer flowers arranged in small gardens shaped as circles, squares, or triangles. The green lawns always looked as if they had just been mowed. Flowers and small berry-bearing bushes were planted along fences and walkways. Evergreens of various sizes surrounded the buildings while crepe myrtles, cherry, dogwood, and Bartlett pear trees were strategically scattered throughout the complexes' grounds, providing flowering trees throughout the seasons. Some areas had benches sitting among bushes, surrounded by evergreens or flowers like lilies. While others, like Thoroughbred Acres, had used natural ponds and streams to create pleasant park areas for its residents to enjoy.

The apartment office and clubhouse sat on the hillside surrounded by a green manicured lawn encircled by a rotary. The tennis courts sat to the left of the rotary. An Olympic-sized pool and a small wading pool with a waterfall were perched slightly above the tennis courts. A sign at the end of the drive where the rotary intersects indicated that all traffic continues to the right.

Sarah went halfway around the rotary and took the drive to her right. Two drives went off the rotary. One went to the apartment buildings where Sarah lived, called the Stables, and the second drive went to the other section, the Paddock. A creek, which flowed into the pond below, separated the two sections. Within minutes, she was inside her apartment building.

The phone rang as she put her key into the door. Throwing her purse into a nearby chair, she ran for the phone in the bedroom. She snatched it before the other party could hang up.

"Hi, honey."

"Hi, sweetie. It's good to hear your voice," Sarah replied.

"Did you go to church this morning?"

"Yes. And then I ate lunch at Vickery Creek, a restaurant at the old Roswell mill. It has really great food. And when you come down here, I'll take you there."

"You'll have that chance next Saturday."

"That'll be great. Not this Saturday? The following Saturday?"

"Right."

"Oh, wonderful!" said Sarah. "You'll get to see your new home here."

"I'm coming down for a meeting in Atlanta. I'm giving a presentation on Monday morning to a prospective client."

"I'll meet you at the airport."

Jason gave Sarah the time and flight number and said he would call her tomorrow night.

"I love you," said Jason.

"I feel your love," replied Sarah. "I love you, sweet man."

They said good-bye, and Sarah put the phone into the receiver with great gladness in her heart. Ginger, a yellow longhair cat, jumped upon the bed; and Sarah, laughing, swooped Ginger up into her arms, exclaiming to her that their man was coming for a visit. Ginger purred softly as Sarah kissed her soft, furry head.

Chapter 3

"It's hot. It's really hot," Alice said aloud to herself as she carried several bags of groceries into the kitchen. It had never been this hot before. The area along the New England coast was always cool in the summer. *It must be that global warming everyone's talking about,* thought Alice. She'd never known it to be ninety-five degrees here, which was the temperature the weatherman announced on this August day. The mansion was cool. Its thick walls kept out the heat.

Alice, a tidy woman in her midfifties with light brown hair showing traces of gray, was the housekeeper for the late Bill Monrose, once owner of the Monrose estate and a multibillion-dollar business. The estate consisted of the three-story mansion and twenty acres that sat along cliffs above the Atlantic Ocean in an area called Beverly Farms, about an hour's drive north of Boston. A six-columned porch spanned the height of the first two stories of the brick home built by Monrose's great-grandfather.

Alice had just finished putting the groceries away when she heard a loud thump, like a chair had fallen over, from the front of the house.

"Ernie, are you here?" shouted Alice. Ernie lived in an apartment over the carriage house on the estate, about a fourth of a mile from the mansion. He was in charge of maintenance and grounds.

Hearing no response, Alice walked through the house to the front hall. She heard some movement and called, "Ernie, is that you?"

"Yes, I'm in here, Alice." Hearing Ernie in the living room, Alice passed from the hall through the living room door.

"Oh, I'm so glad to see you moving those cases out from the wall. Now I can clean behind them." Thick blond hair capped his tanned, trim five-foot-eight frame. Perspiration trickled down his forehead. His hands rested on a hand truck. The five cases, with sides and doors made of glass, stood six feet tall. Each contained six glass shelves. Bill had them specially made to show off his collection of knickknacks from his travels around the world.

"Glad to do it for you. I noticed you have all the stuff packed in boxes. I hope Elliot's not going to sell them."

"Not that I know of. I put them in boxes so they wouldn't get broken when you moved the cases. Also, I cleaned each one carefully. Many of these beauties are worth thousands of dollars and I don't want to break any of them."

"Bill certainly has a great collection of china, jewelry, and whatnots from other countries. He told me how he came upon some of them," Ernie commented. "Interesting stories."

"They are lovely," Alice sighed.

"Let me know when you're finished in here, and I'll move them back for you." He paused a moment, then, "Don't you want to get some help in here to clean this place? It's a lot for you to do by yourself. I'm sure Mr. Winter will give his OK to it."

"I'm sure he would, but I want to do it. It helps relieve my grief. I didn't think I would carry on for anyone after my Bert died. It took me a while to get over Bert's passing."

"Well, you and Mr. Monrose were close friends these last five or so years, if you don't mind my saying so."

"You're right. I tried to keep our relationship professional, but that was getting hard to do. Bill was a really nice person. Too bad his nephew gave him such a hard time. Bill and his sister tried to bring him up right after his dad died."

"I wonder what Elliot's going to do with this place. It and the business are his now."

"I overheard him talking to Larry Abbott, Mr. Bill's attorney, when they were both in the library on Saturday, going through some of Mr. Bill's personal business files. Elliot was asking what the place would bring in the real estate market. Mr. Abbot questioned why he was asking, was he going to sell the place? I heard Elliot say he was thinking about it. But Elliot did say that would be the last resort because he enjoyed this place very much," said Alice.

"Humm. I hope he doesn't. But if he does keep the place, I'm not sure I would stay. I don't think I could work for him."

"I don't trust him," said Alice.

"Do you think Elliot knows anything about the other safe?"

"No. Mr. Bill made sure Elliot was never around when he opened it."

"That's good. So the only one he knows about is in the study," reflected Ernie. "You know Mr. Bill expected us to keep that second safe a secret."

"I know we both will," commented Alice. "Elliot won't get anything from me about anything in this house."

"You sure don't like him."

"I try to like him, but it's hard."

"Has he said anything to you about moving in?"

"No. But he does have some of his clothes here since, as you know, he's here on weekends."

"I guess we'll have to wait and see. Is there anything else you would like me to move before I leave?"

"No, there isn't," replied Alice.

"I'll be in the carriage house if you need me. I need to do maintenance on the riding mower and the two gas mowers. I'm also putting in an air conditioner in my apartment. I got the last one they had at the appliance store. Very few stores have air conditioners you know. Summers have always been cool." He wiped the sweat from his forehead with his handkerchief and started for the living room door, pushing the hand truck in front of him.

"That's good. I know you'll be cool tonight. And thank you," Alice called to him as he went through the living room into the front hall. She heard the side door open and close. She looked through one of the living room windows and watched him push the hand truck through the garden on his way to the carriage house.

I'm glad he's around. I know Ernie misses Mr. Bill. Men have a different way of grieving than we women do. Alice went to the kitchen and prepared herself lunch. *I'll clean the living room and the library afterward.*

As Alice put her lunch together, she thought about Elliot. *Such a contrast to his cousin Sarah, a beautiful and sensible woman happily married to Jason Edmonds. Not that Elliot wasn't handsome. He was and he knew it.* Anyway, she knew Mr. Bill wanted Sarah to take over the family business when he was ready to retire. Bill would speak about it from time to time with her and told her Sarah had turned down his request to take over the business when he retired or died. He never did say why Sarah turned him down. Alice also suspected Elliot harbored a resentment toward Jason for marrying Sarah.

Bill's death came as a shock. She remembered Mr. Bill had not come down to breakfast that morning. He always ate breakfast at six during the week. When he had not made an appearance by six fifteen, Alice called him on the intercom from the kitchen. He hadn't answered. She sensed something wrong and called Ernie. Together they went to Mr. Bill's room and found him lying on the floor next to his bed. She called to him but he gave no response. She felt for a pulse but hadn't found any. His wrist and neck were cold. Ernie tried too. She couldn't believe he was gone. The medics who answered their call said he was dead. The rest was a blur. Later, she learned that his death was ruled as heart failure. Alice wondered how could that be. He was a healthy man of fifty-nine years. She remembered how elated Bill was about the clean bill of health his doctor had given him two months before he died.

Something was wrong. Alice couldn't put her finger on it. She shared her thoughts with Ernie. His response to her was that she watched too many mysteries on TV.

Chapter 4

After Sarah took her morning walk around the apartment grounds, she settled down to finish typing the conversation she had with Adie Appleton about her childhood days. She enjoyed her sessions with Adie, who was ninety-two years young. Her mind was sharp, and she kept up with what was going on around her. Sarah had been told that it was Adie who led a community drive to provide a shelter for the homeless four years ago. Adie was still driving her own car at that time and made a number of trips to the town hall, local stores, and shopping centers to inform the town's citizens about the need for the shelter. Adie got it built; and last year, it had been expanded to include some units for homeless families.

Sarah sat down at the word processor and turned on the tape recorder. When Adie's voice started talking, Sarah began typing. She stopped the recorder every four or five minutes, sometimes rewinding it to catch a word or phase, then continued typing.

Sarah had been working for almost three hours when the phone rang, startling her. Picking it up, she recognized Mrs. Greyson's voice.

"I hope I'm not bothering you, my dear," said Mrs. Greyson, "but I noticed some strangers outside. If you look out your window, you can see two cars. One is a green Toyota Camry parked by Building B and the other is a red Ford van, which just pulled into the space in front of my building. Do you see what the guy in the Camry has in his hands?" Sarah went out on the porch with the portable phone.

"It looks like a tackle box." She spoke in a whisper so her voice won't carry. "Maybe they're going fishing. Why are you interested?"

As Sarah spoke, the man from the Toyota walked over to the red van and got in.

"I'll tell you in a minute. Can you see what they're doing? I can't see much from here."

Sarah watched, as the guy with the tackle box lifted a tray out of it and brought out what looked like an envelope. All she could see of the other guy was his hand holding a brown bag. The bag was taken by the guy with the tackle box.

"What's going on?" asked Mrs. Greyson.

"Just wait a minute."

The guy put the bag in his tackle box. He stepped out of the van and went to his car. He got in and left in a hurry.

"It looks like the guy with the tackle box gave an envelope to the guy in the van. He in turn gave him a brown bag. Think it's fishing worms?"

"Maybe yes, maybe no," responded Mrs. Greyson. "My grandson said the police suspects that this place is being used as a drop-off for drug dealers. I just happened to be standing at the window when I saw those two pull in. I've never seen the red van or the green car here before. I got both their license numbers and I'll check with the office to see if the cars belong to anyone here."

"The red van is leaving. Let me know what you find out. I hope no one here is involved in the drug business. It's hard to believe they would make their transactions in broad daylight."

"It is, but Veny says they work in the open because very few people pay any attention to what is going on around them. They feel safe in a crowd. Would you tell my grandson what you saw if he asks?"

"Yeah, I'll help. But it was probably a bag of fishing worms the guy bought," said Sarah. "I don't want to think this place is being used by drug dealers for their dirty business."

"I don't either. I'll let you know what I find out. Keep your eyes open, dear."

"OK," said Sarah as Mrs. Greyson hung up her phone.

Sarah didn't like the thought of drugs being right here. She hoped the bag was full of fishing worms.

Chapter 5

Chris was busy fixing another pot of coffee when Larry called to her from his office.

"I can't believe it's Thursday already. Bring your pad and pen. We've got some letters that need to go out today."

"I'll be there when I get the coffee going," Chris replied.

She waited for the coffee to start dripping into the pot before she moved to her desk. Chris found a pen and then picked up her shorthand book.

After dictating several letters to Chris, Larry told her to make sure they got out in the morning's mail.

"Also," he added, "straighten up the client's files. I couldn't find several of the folders when I was going through the cabinet last night."

"They should be in order, sir. However, I could have put a few of the new files in the wrong place," Chris responded. "You know that we have been pretty busy preparing for the Redmon trial."

"You're doing OK," Larry commented. "But we need to be more careful with our files."

Three visitors and a number of phone calls later, Chris came into Larry's office with a large envelope.

"Sir, I was working on the files to make sure they were in order when I dropped a folder. It landed beside the file cabinet on the floor next to the wall. While I was picking it up, I noticed a corner of this envelope sticking out from behind the cabinet. It must have fallen out of the in-mail basket that was set on top of the cabinet. It has been back there for a while. Notice the date of the postmark. I'm going to move the in-mail basket so this wouldn't happen again."

"Gosh, that's the day before Bill died," Larry uttered in amazement. "Have we missed any other mail?"

"None that I know of."

"Find a place for that basket where mail can't drop behind it. And thank you for finding this. It makes me wonder if the cleaning people are really doing their job. Seems like they should have found it while they were cleaning."

Larry recognized the handwriting on the envelope. He told her he didn't want to take any calls and to cancel his next appointment. It was late in the afternoon, and Larry wanted some quiet time with his old buddy's letter. Larry had been Bill's attorney ever since he passed the bar exam many years ago. They had become steadfast friends over the years. Bill's sudden death threw him for a loop. His last conversation with Bill concerned a change Bill was making in his will regarding his nephew, Elliot.

When Chris left his office, Larry closed the door. It was disquieting to look at Bill's handwriting after all these months.

Two hours later, Larry was still sitting at his desk with documents in his hands. *What a bombshell*, he thought. He was surprised. Not that Bill had disinherited Elliot. He knew Bill was upset with his nephew. The surprise was to whom Bill had left the bulk of his estate and why.

Even though he knew the codicil Bill added to his will was legal, he thought he had better check it out with Dee, a former law partner who specialized in wills. They had parted ways because Dee's friends were questionable. Some definitely were on the shady side of the law. Larry picked up the phone and keyed in the number.

"This is Larry. I would like to speak to Dee. Tell him it's important."

Larry waited a few minutes.

"Dee, hello."

"Yes. Would you have time to look over a codicil that just came to me this afternoon?"

A response on the other line prompted Bill to ask, "Can I come over in about an hour? Fine, I'll see you then."

After Dee looked over the codicil, Larry and Dee spent time talking shop and catching up on what each was doing. Their visit was interrupted by a call from Dee's wife, reminding him to pick up a few items from the grocery store on the way home. Larry got up and moved toward the door to leave. Dee motioned for him to wait. After a few more minutes of conversation, Dee hung up the phone and said he enjoyed Larry's visit, then escorted him to the office door were they shook hands. Larry headed for the elevator as Dee returned to his office to lock up for the night.

Larry stopped by his office on his way home and left Bill's documents in a safe. Dee verified the codicil was legitimate and would hold up in court in case Elliot decided to contest it.

Bill had included a birth certificate signed by him and the child's mother and a letter written by him, which was notarized, and a few other documents. Thinking Elliot may try to prove the birth certificate a phony, Larry employed Don, a part-time investigator, to check the hospital records. Don would call him in the morning with what he would find out.

"Not much else to do right now. Guess I'll stop somewhere for supper. Then home," Larry said aloud to himself. Chris had gone home before he left for Dee's office. He turned out the light on his desk and then clicked off the wall switch connected to the ceiling light before closing the door to his office. Larry made sure the outer door to his office was locked before he headed down the hall to the elevator.

Chapter 6

Jason enjoyed strolling through the gardens on his way to work. The company that employed him had their offices in a brownstone on Commonwealth Avenue. Today, Jason decided to take the train and ride the Green Line to Park Street. He was thinking of Sarah, remembering the many times they ambled together through the commons and the gardens. Sometimes in the summer after work, they would come here and ride on the Swan boats. Then they would wander to the Globe Bookstore, browsing through books until they were hungry.

Jason missed her and wondered what Sarah was doing about now. *I'll be seeing her next Saturday, but I'll call her when I get to the office,* he thought. It was Friday—his day to buy donuts for the office. He stopped at Maggie's Donut Shop and bought a box of donut holes iced in different flavors.

Charlene, the office receptionist, was on the phone when he came through the reception area. He held up the bag of donut holes for her to see and pointed toward the back. Jason took them into the breakroom, shouting, "Donuts everyone, donuts."

The breakroom was once the kitchen when the building was a single-family home. Now remodeled, it was a combination snack area and communications room. The bay window, which looked out over an alley, held a table and four chairs. Opposite the counter and refrigerator was a copier. Sitting on a long table were two laser printers and a fax machine.

Jason poured himself a cup of coffee and took a few of the holes in a napkin upstairs to his office. Jason called out, "donuts, donuts" as he went down the hall.

The phone was ringing as Jason entered his office. He quickly set down the coffee and picked up the phone with his free hand.

"Hello, Mr. Abbot," Jason replied. "Just a minute, while I put these . . . ahh . . . these down." He switched the phone to his other ear. "I'm doing fine, thank you. And you? . . . Sarah is doing all right. I'm going to Atlanta next weekend and visit with her. Some business too . . . this afternoon? Just a minute and let me check."

Jason called to his assistant to see if he had any appointments for the afternoon. She informed him that he had a 1:30 appointment and a 2:15.

"Mr. Abbot, I'll probably be free after three o'clock this afternoon. Can you tell me what this is about? . . . OK. I'll see you then at 3:30."

Jason wondered what was on Mr. Abbott's mind. He hadn't talked to him since the reading of Sarah's Uncle Bill's will.

"Send Mr. Edmonds in," Larry told Chris.

"Good to see you, Jason. I would like to have Sarah here but I know it is impossible for her to be here on such a short notice. There have been some new developments concerning Bill Monrose's estate. A codicil written by Bill Monrose the day before he died has been found. Before we go on any further, I would like Sarah to hear what I have to say. Larry pressed the intercom on his phone.

"Chris, do you have Sarah on the line?"

"Yes. Do you want me to put her through now?"

"Please do." Larry pushed the button marked speaker.

"Hello, Sarah," said Larry.

"Hello, Mr. Abbot. It's a surprise to hear from you. Is everything all right?"

"It all depends on how you look at it. By the way, Jason is here."

"Hi, Jason!" responded Sarah. "You know what's going on?"

"No. I got here only a few minutes ago," Jason replied.

"Sarah, Bill has left a codicil to his will which was recently found. It's dated the day before he died," Larry explained. "It's very legal, and I require your presence for the reading of it."

"Is anyone else named on it?"

"Yes there is. When do you think you can get here?" Larry asked.

Jason interrupted, "Well, she can come back with me next Tuesday. The following week."

"Can you move it up to Monday of that week?"

"Well, yes," said Jason. "Sarah, how about you? Can you come back with me on Monday?"

"I sure can."

"Then it's set. I'll tell Chris to put you down for four o'clock a week from this Monday afternoon. If your plane is late, give me a call and we'll reschedule for that evening," Larry told Jason and Sarah.

"Sarah, I'll be seeing you then."

"Right. And I'll see you, Jason, next Saturday," said Sarah.

"Good-bye, honey," said Jason.

Larry hung up the phone.

"There are some things you both need to know but I'm going to wait till next Monday to tell you. It's best I tell you both at the same time," Larry stated. "And it's something that can't be discussed during a conference call. I wish we could do this sooner, but it will give me time to contact the other party involved in the change."

"From what you're saying, I'm gathering that the codicil may be in Sarah's favor. If so, I'm wondering why."

"Well, you have between now and our meeting to wonder," said Larry with a smile. "It was good of you to come here on such a short notice." Both Larry and Jason got up from their chairs and moved toward the door.

"You're leaving me with a lot of questions." Jason stood in the doorway of Larry's office hoping Larry would tell him more but Larry didn't.

"They'll be answered at our meeting. Give Sarah my best when you see her."

"I will, and thank you," Jason said as he shook Larry's hand.

Larry closed the door to his office as Jason turned to leave. He had some thinking to do.

Standing in front of the building where he had just spoken to Larry, Jason turned to go to his office. *Just about everyone at the office is leaving for home now,* thought Jason. *I'll call it a day too. I'll call Sarah from home.* Jason turned around and headed for the Park Street station.

A foreboding suddenly darkened Jason's thoughts. A shiver went down his spine. Was the sensation connected to the change in the will? Jason wondered as he strolled along the street toward the Common. Was there some evil mischief going on, affecting someone close to him? Jason didn't have a premonition often. He called it premonition for a lack of a better word. Whenever Jason had one, someone close to him was in trouble. Sometimes he would be the object of the ominous activity. He recalled he had a similar feeling before Sarah's car accident several years ago. *Was she the object of evil activity this time? Did the codicil have anything to do with it?*

The sound of a car horn close by broke into Jason's thoughts. He was in front of a white sedan whose frustrated driver was telling him to get out of the street for "couldn't he see the light was green?"

Jason jumped quickly on the curb and the driver drove by yelling obscenities at him. *I better watch where I'm going,* thought Jason. *Better get home and call Sarah.*

Jason had strayed in his walk to the commons and was now standing on a corner of a street that borders an area referred to as "no man's land." It consisted of several blocks close to Boston's downtown area that catered to shady businesses—and characters. He spotted the familiar Orange Line logo a half block away. It would take him to the North Station as well as the Green Line.

———————

Larry needed to inform Elliot of the events. It was the end of the workweek. He could call Elliot tomorrow. But since Jason and Sarah knew something was up, he might as well tell Elliot as soon as possible.

"Chris," he called from the door. "Please get Mr. Winter on the phone."

Chapter 7

Jason opened the door to a ringing phone. He noticed the mail on the floor where the mailman had pushed it through the slot. He scooped it up, ran into the dining room, threw the mail on the dining room table as he passed by, and picked up the phone.

"Hello," he shouted, breathless.

"Did you just get in?" Sarah's voice asked.

"Hi, honey. And yes, I just got in. I was going to call you as soon as I went through the mail. I'm glad you called," said Jason.

"It's good to hear your voice, sweet man," Sarah replied.

"Aawwah, honey, I miss you. That sure was some conversation with Larry."

"It sure was. Since I'm to be at the reading, does it mean I'm going to receive more than what I have, or receive nothing?"

"I don't know. It's a puzzle. I couldn't get any more out of Larry after the phone call. He said I'll have to wait till our meeting."

"Do you think Elliot will be there?" Sarah asked.

"I would think so."

"Does he want you to sit in on the reading?"

"He didn't say. But it sounds like it, doesn't it."

"Yes, it does."

"I guess it's best not to waste our time speculating about Uncle Bill's codicil. We will know soon enough what's in it," said Jason.

"You're right, sweetie."

"Well, I'll get my return flight changed and get a ticket for you. How long do you want to stay?"

"Oh, I haven't thought of that. I can probably stay for a week. Maybe longer. And I'll bring Ginger. So make sure that she can fly in the cabin with me. I don't want her flying in cargo with the luggage."

Fifteen more minutes of conversation, then Jason hung up the phone. He was delighted Ginger was returning with them. Jason missed the nosy feline. He missed her sleeping in the bed and getting in his way when he brought groceries into the house. Talking with Sarah eased the anxiety, but the premonition was still with him.

Chapter 8

Sarah was awakened by a noise. She sat up in bed, listening for what awakened her. It was quiet. The digital clock read 2:15 AM. *Humm. It's early,* thought Sarah, half-asleep.

A few minutes had gone by when she thought she heard someone outside. Curious, Sarah got up, grabbed her robe, and pulled it around her. She peeked through the blind but didn't notice anything. *I'll go out to the porch for a better view.*

As Sarah went through the bedroom door, Ginger jumped off the bed and followed her. Sarah opened the sliding glass door quietly, and she and Ginger went out to the porch. Sarah listened for about ten minutes. She turned around, ready to go in, when she heard a voice. Sarah scanned the cars parked across from her building. A streetlight silhouetted figures against a van, and she could hear voices talking softly.

One of them yelled and the other told him to be quiet. "You blew it, you bastard," he shouted.

By this time, Sarah had seated herself in a chair close to the screen in hopes she might see the faces of the voices without being seen. Ginger was exploring the porch.

A sudden crash behind Sarah startled her. She jumped up to see where it came from. She saw Ginger's tail retreating through the sliding door. The potted fern was not in its place on the flower cart: it was on the floor with dirt scattered everywhere.

Oh no. Ginger had been in the fern. Probably was going to take a nibble or two.

One of the men below shone a flashlight on the walls of her apartment building. Sarah ducked to the floor, hoping she escaped the light as it swept her porch.

What seemed like five minutes passed, when Sarah heard a car speed up the street. She waited for a few minutes before looking. The van was gone.

Well, I'm wide-awake now, thought Sarah as she stooped to pick up the fern. *I'll clean this up later. Might as well have a glass of milk.* She placed the potted fern on the cart and went to the kitchen.

Sarah sat in the recliner in the living room while she drank the milk, thinking over what she saw and heard a little while ago. She would call Mrs. Greyson later this morning and tell her about the latest events.

Feeling drowsy, Sarah went to bed. A little later, a soft small yellow body of fur jumped upon the bed and curled up next to her.

Sarah awoke to the bright August sun glowing through the cracks of the blinds. *I don't want to sleep this late,* she thought to herself. *Oh well, it's Saturday.*

Chapter 9

This morning, Elliot drove to Monrose. He called Elaine and told her he has business to take care of and wouldn't be meeting her at the club for their usual Saturday round of tennis. Even though Elaine was used to Elliot canceling at the last minute, this time she was a little put out with him, which Elliot sensed over the phone. *Well,* thought Elliot, *I have more important things to take care of right now. I'll see her this evening.*

Although he was concerned with where he was going to raise the rest of the money he needed by next week, Elliot took pleasure in the drive to Monrose. It was a gorgeous August morning with a hint of fall in the air. Elliot loved the fall season. The sun's rays were glistening on the water, making the ocean look like white crystals. For a while, he forgot his financial plight until he saw the gate to Monrose looming up on the right side of the road. Elliot's dilemma flooded his thought and the tranquility he'd savored only minutes before was obliterated and replaced by apprehension.

Monrose Mansion is set high above the ocean on a cliff. The drive circled in front of the house. Another drive leads off to the left shortly after entering the gate. This drive went to the stables and the carriage house.

Closer to the house, another drive took off to the right and went alongside the house. Tall shrubbery at the end of the drive prevented cars from running off the cliff into the ocean. Alice parked her car there since it was close to the entrance that leads to her room and the kitchen.

Elliot admired the facade of Monrose as he drove his car part way around the circle. He stopped in front of the mansion. It was highlighted by a Doric portico of six white columns, almost the height of the three-story brick house. The portico, reached by a short flight of granite steps, shielded a wide fan-lighted central doorway. Elliot took pleasure in the portico floor inlaid with gray marble. He preferred the gray marble over the pink, which was on the back porch and the sunroom floor. The architect's design of the house pleased

Elliot. As he opened the front door, Elliot's thoughts turned to the matter at hand—selling Bill's treasures.

Elliot had a copy of the inventory list made by the group Mr. Abbott had hired. A few items were worth a lot of money, especially to collectors. His visit was to determine if he could sell them before his deadline with Henry. He arranged to meet with Mr. Leonard Jewel, an antique collector and owner of the most prestigious antique store in the area, here this morning.

Alice had let Mr. Jewel in and seated him in the study. Mr. Jewel was a tall man who took pains with what he considered the "proper look" for a person knowledgeable in antiquities. He always wore a three-piece suit with a watch chain dangling from his vest pocket. The watch was a beautiful piece of art, which Mr. Jewel had found among the jewelry of an estate he was consigned to sell. He sold all the jewelry but the watch. Mr. Jewel couldn't part with it, especially when he found out what it was worth. So he held on to it for his "retirement fund," as he put it. Since he enjoyed looking at it often, he wore the watch in his vest pocket instead of locking it away in a safe.

Alice met Elliot at the front door.

"Mr. Jewel is in the study," she informed Elliot. "Shall I serve you coffee?"

"Thank you," replied Elliot. "But not right now."

He then proceeded to the study. Mr. Jewel was looking at his pocket watch when Elliot entered the room. "I'm Elliot Winter," extending his hand forward to Mr. Jewel. Mr. Jewel slipped the watch into his pocket and took Elliot's hand.

"Glad you're on time, Mr. Winter. This is a most lovely home."

"Thank you," murmured Elliot.

"Well, I gathered from our brief conversation on the phone you have a few items in which I might be interested."

"Yes, there are a few articles my uncle has left me that I want to sell. If it wasn't for the tight financial circumstances I'm in right now, I wouldn't sell them."

"Let me see what you have."

"The items are in the display cases in the living room."

Elliot led the way to the living room while Mr. Jewel followed, looking at everything along the way with an appraising eye. Elliot sensed Mr. Jewel was making mental notes of items he would like to see in his shop, calculating the dollar amount for each one he sold.

Mr. Jewel's eyes gleamed with delight at the two Chinese vases Elliot showed him and the two rare editions of Eden's *Holcomb Pond*. The collection contained 217 items, according to the inventory. Several of the depressed glass pieces were valued at $10,000 each. The items were kept in locked, displayed cases made of glass. Each stood six feet tall, containing six glass shelves. Five cases were scattered around the living room, and one sat in the middle of the library.

"Do you want to do get a better look at the jewelry in this case?"

"Yes, I would appreciate it," Mr. Jewel replied.

Elliot unlocked the display case and handed Mr. Jewel several of the pieces inlaid with diamonds and rubies. Elliot didn't say anything. He just watched Mr. Jewel. He knew by the man's expression that he had a gold mine.

Finally, Mr. Jewel put on his business face and asked, "How much do you want for this collection?"

Elliot thought about this for a few minutes then replied, "Eight hundred and fifty thousand dollars." *This amount, along with the amount I skimmed from Monrose Industries, will be more than enough to repay Henry*, Elliot mused.

"No," said Mr. Jewel, "that's more than I'm prepared to pay."

"Then what are you prepared to pay?"

"Six hundred thousand dollars."

"No. You know that this collection is worth more than that." Both men were resolute. They had come to an impasse. Elliot could tell Mr. Jewel wanted the collection, but the man just didn't want to pay much for it. Mr. Jewel was thinking he could mark up the price of each item, probably by 75 percent.

Elliot needed money, but he wasn't going to sell the collection for less than what it was worth. "There are other dealers," Elliot told him. He turned to leave the room, when Mr. Jewel said, "Mr. Winter, I'll give you what you asked. But I'll not be able to get the money to you until Saturday."

Elliot thought he might as well forget the deal since he needed to give the money to Henry on Thursday. He'll call Henry and ask if he would wait till the weekend for his money.

"Mr. Jewel, I need the money before the weekend. Let me think this over. Please wait here while I call my advisor." Elliot then went to the study and called Henry.

Elliot knew Henry didn't like to be bothered on Saturdays for any reason. He called anyway, thinking all they could do was kill him. Elliot shuddered at the thought.

Henry's assistant answered. Elliot asked to speak to Henry. A few minutes later, an angry Henry shouted over the phone. Elliot explained the reason he called. Henry started shouting again, and then Elliot heard someone in the background talking to Henry. He then told Elliot he could pay the rest of the money to him on Sunday. "But you'd better have half the money to me on Thursday," shouted Henry.

"I'll have half of the money to you by Thursday," Elliot promised.

"And don't you ever bother me on Saturday again." Elliot heard the phone click and then the dial tone. *Not exactly what I wanted, but it will have to do.*

Elliot returned to Mr. Jewel in the living room who was sitting in a wing-back chair holding a Faberge egg, admiring the handiwork. He cringed and hurried across the room to Mr. Jewel.

"Mr. Jewel, let me put that back in the display case." Elliot took the egg and placed it carefully in the case. "Saturday will be all right. Do you plan to pick up the collection when you bring the check with you?"

"Yes. I'll have a truck to pick up the items Saturday morning. I'll be here a little before then with the check. I'll call you with the time." While they talked, Elliot escorted Mr. Jewel to the front door.

"Thank you, Mr. Jewel. I'll see you then." Shaking hands with Mr. Jewel, Elliot opened the front door. Mr. Jewel smiled and nodded before turning toward his Mercedes.

Now, thought Elliot, *all I have to do is make sure Alice and Ernie aren't here next Saturday morning.*

Chapter 10

Sarah rolled out of bed and went into the kitchen to put the coffee on. Ginger was right behind her, meowing for some food.

"You shouldn't get any breakfast after knocking over the fern this morning. But you are a good girl otherwise."

Sarah picked up Ginger and held her close while stroking her silky fur. Ginger purred loudly. She fed Ginger her usual fish-flavored cat food and sat down with her cup of coffee at the dining room table, which sat in a small area off the living room, overlooking the screened porch.

After eating toast and cereal with the second cup of coffee, she called Mrs. Greyson. Her voicemail informed Sarah she wasn't available and requested in a pleasant voice to leave a message and phone number. "This is Sarah. I'll call you later. This is Saturday morning."

I wonder what Jason's doing, Sarah thought to herself. While she was dressing, she thought of their townhouse in Salem and the dreams they had when they leased it seven years ago. A year later, they had purchased it and, three years ago, turned the basement into two rooms, a complete bath, and several closets.

Sarah thought of their rambles around Salem, visits to the Essex and Peabody Museums and the delicious meals they ate at Weylu's at the Essex Mall. She missed him. *It's going to be a wonderful weekend.* They'd go to the old mill in Roswell for lunch or supper. *It's going to be great.*

One of the things she needed to do today was to find the best route to the airport. It had been a year since she'd driven there, and that was from Buckhead.

Sarah was brought from her thoughts by the telephone ringing. Ginger thought it was the doorbell and ran to the door. Sarah was laughing when she picked up the phone.

"Oh hello, Mrs. Greyson. I'm just laughing at this crazy cat."

"I had just returned a few minutes ago from the grocery store," Mrs. Greyson volunteered. "What's up?"

"I want to tell you what happened early this morning. Did you hear any noise outside?"

"No, I can't say that I did. I slept very well."

Sarah told Mrs. Greyson the events of the early morning hours. Mrs. Greyson advised her to call her grandson. Sarah wasn't sure, but Mrs. Greyson persuaded her to call Veny.

"On second thought, I'll call him," she said. "Since you two haven't met, it might be better if he calls you." Sarah consented with indifference.

Chapter 11

A gray Mercedes sped up the ramp from Highway 62, pausing only a few seconds before joining the whizzing traffic on Highway 128. The driver was ecstatic with his new acquisitions. Even though Mr. Jewel regretted paying more than he wanted on the Monrose collection, he knew his profit would be double, maybe triple, of his capital outlay.

Picking up the cell phone, Mr. Jewel dialed his bank. Once on the line, he asked for Ben Wall.

"Hello, Ben. I'm acquiring some exquisite antiques, and I want you to transfer funds from my money market account to the store account. I would like you to take care of it as quickly as possible."

Mr. Jewel told Ben the amount he want transferred and instructed him to have a cashier's check waiting for him to pick up Friday morning. He would call Mr. Winter when he receives the check and arrange to pick up the collection on Saturday.

His next call was to a longtime client who wanted an original edition of Eden's *Holcomb Pond*. The client was delighted to hear one was available and offered more for the copy than Mr. Jewel had planned to ask. Mr. Jewel told him that would be fine and he could pick it up next week at the store.

Whizzing down the highway with the rest of the cars, vans, and trucks, Mr. Jewel moved his Mercedes from the left to the right lane. In a few more minutes, Mr. Jewel would be exiting off Highway 128 onto the ramp that led to Route 1. He was talking to Mrs. Phipps about the vases, as his Mercedes came parallel with Route 1. Paying more attention to the conversation than the road, he didn't notice the trailer truck coming up on his left as he pulled onto Route 1 from the ramp. There was the sound of skidding tires, shattering glass and ripping metal as the Mercedes and truck collided.

Chapter 12

Well, what do I say now? The first paragraph is good. Huumm. I'll tell them how my experience fits in with the job description they gave in the ad, reflected Sarah. "I do not like writing cover letters," Sarah said to Ginger who was lying on the bed. "What a way to spend my Saturday." Three cover letters were laid on the bed next to a folder marked "resumes." Next to the folder were four letters of rejection for employment. Sarah's thoughts about the cover letter were interrupted by the doorbell ringing.

"Wonder who? Oh, it's probably Mrs. Greyson's grandson," said Sarah to the air.

"Who is it?" Sara shouted as she approached the door.

"Officer Greyson. My grandmom asked me to talk to you."

Sarah opened the door. She recognized Mrs. Greyson's green eyes in the face of the tall, young uniformed man standing in front of her. She could see the family resemblance.

"I'm glad to meet you."

"Grandmom told me what you heard and saw earlier this morning. I would appreciate it if you tell me in your own words what happened," Officer Greyson stated.

"I'll be glad to. Please come in. But first, would you like some coffee or tea?"

"Oh no, thank you," he replied.

"Well then, let's sit down."

Officer Greyson went over to the sofa and sat down close to Ginger's usual sleeping place. But Officer Greyson didn't know this. He pulled out his notebook and pen and flipped open the notebook. Sarah sat in a lounge chair opposite him.

"Mrs. Edmonds, would you just tell me from the time you awoke what you saw and heard."

Sarah and Officer Greyson were finishing with the interview when Ginger came slowly wandering out of the kitchen where she'd been eating. Ginger made a run for the sofa. Within a few feet from Officer Greyson, she stopped suddenly and stared at him. Ginger then half arched her back and with stiff legs moved closer to investigate this strange person sitting close to her sleeping place. She relaxed her back and began sniffing. She jumped on the sofa next to him and sniffed his shirtsleeve then proceeded to put her front paws on his leg to continue sniffing at his shirt.

"Ginger," said Sarah, "you leave our guest alone." Sarah raised from her chair to remove Ginger from Officer Greyson's lap.

"Oh, this is all right," he said. "She's curious. I like cats and dogs. She probably smells Kelley, our police dog, on me. I had him on patrol this morning."

Officer Greyson petted Ginger, who immediately began purring and laid down in his lap.

"If you don't mind, I'll take you up on your offer of coffee. I'll take some time to get acquainted with Ginger, right?"

"Right, Ginger is her name. We're not keeping you from your work?" Sarah inquired.

"No, I'll count this as my afternoon break," said Officer Greyson.

"Ginger, you may have gotten your roommate into some trouble this morning."

Sarah brought him coffee and herself a Diet Coke.

"Grandmom is very fond of you. And I can see why. She's upset about the drug situation in this area. Grandmom's happy you feel the same way she does about keeping drugs out of the apartment complex." Smiling, he continued, "She describes you two as partners in crime prevention. But all kidding aside, if these guys are in the drug business, it's best to stay clear of them. Some of them are pretty mean," Officer Greyson said.

"Well, I feel close to your grandmother. She's a good friend and very helpful in showing me around Roswell. And about those guys, I'll stay clear. This morning was as close as I want to get to them," Sarah said.

Officer Greyson finished his coffee and put the cup and saucer on the table next to the sofa. He gently lifted the purring, half-asleep Ginger off his lap and laid her on the sofa next to him. Ginger got up, turned around, and closed her eyes as she lay down.

As Officer Greyson left, with a grin, he said, "Mrs. Edmonds, you and Grandmom don't go arresting those guys. Seriously, though, give me a call if they show up again. You have my number. I told Grandmom the same thing."

"I will," Sarah responded. "Good-bye."

"Good-bye, and thanks for the coffee."

Chapter 13

This is wonderful, this is great, thought Elliot as he watched Mr. Jewel drive away in his Mercedes. *Now I have all the money Henry has demanded plus extra for me.* But it was close. What would he have done if Mr. Jewel hadn't bought the collection? Well, he did and that was that. He felt free for the first time in weeks.

Elliot went to look for Alice. He found her in the dining room, polishing silver.

"Alice, the plumbers will be here on Tuesday to work on the toilet in Uncle Bill's bathroom. I noticed the other day that the leak behind the toilet is worse. I remember Uncle Bill mentioning it the day before he died, so I checked it, and it does need attention. Let me know if they give you any trouble or they don't arrive by ten o'clock."

Alice replied that she'd take care of them.

"And I've decided to spend the night here. Don't worry about getting any meals for me. I'll take care of myself. Is there any bacon and eggs?"

"Yes," replied Alice, "I went to the grocery yesterday and loaded up the refrigerator and pantry. Something told me I might have some company over the weekend."

"That's great. I might invite a guest for supper tonight," Elliot said as he left the dining room.

Alice thought Elliot was the happiest person she had seen for quite a while. Happier than when he learned he had inherited most of his uncle's estate. The talk with that gentleman this morning did him a lot of good, she thought. *I wonder what they talked about? Well,* reasoned Alice, *if it's for me to know, Elliot will surely tell me.*

Alice thought after she has finished polishing the silver she would let Ernie know Elliot was staying for the night. Elliot may want Ernie to do some errands for him this afternoon.

Elliot wandered out onto the back porch and watched the waves hit the rocks below as the tide came in. He cared for Monrose. *It's going to be great living*

here. I'll have more good times, like my grandparents when they lived here. They knew how to enjoy life. Once he paid Henry off, he would have no more dealings with him. He would stay away from his gambling establishments. Elliot reasoned Monrose Industries had enough money he could use to open his own casino. Maybe his establishments could even rival Henry's. Now that he was head of the business, he could find a way to support some of his contraband activities through it. Maybe some dummy corporations. Then again, he could sell some of the entities and pocket some of the proceeds for his personal use.

Yes, it's going to be great living here, thought Elliot. *It's time to settle down and get married. Elaine is the choice.* Mother would be happy about that. If he could get Elaine to bed with him. He had not been successful so far. He needed to convince Elaine to marry him. He knew that she knew about his embezzlement. She had installed the finance account security system under Bill's direction, and he knew she reported his indiscretion to Bill. As far as he could tell, Elaine didn't know he knew. He wondered if she had told anyone else. By marrying her, his secret would be safe because a wife couldn't be forced to testify against her husband. And if he was accused, he could probably make it look as if Elaine was helping him with the embezzlement. Or better yet, he could make it look as if she was the embezzler. If she refused to marry him, Elaine must go. He didn't relish the idea, but he couldn't leave any loose ends. Elaine was so much like Sarah. He loved Sarah at one time. *Maybe I still do,* Elliot reflected. He was attracted to Elaine. From what he could tell, she was attracted to him. But she kept a tight rein on her emotions. The toughest part for him was keeping Elaine from meeting Sarah. He made sure no one was at the mansion when Elaine visited. The wedding would be the best time for them to meet.

Elaine was upset with him, as was her team, when he closed down the finance account security system. He fired her three-member team and moved her to another project. Elaine turned in her resignation, but he talked her into staying.

"I'd better call Elaine and invite her out here tonight," he said aloud. *Maybe she won't be mad.* Elliot could tell Elaine was ticked off this morning when he canceled their tennis date.

Pulling himself away from the ocean and the porch, Elliot went to the study. He sat down at the desk and noticed a piece of paper under the corner of the blotter. Elliot keyed in the club's number and started to look around for a pencil so he could doodle while he talked. He opened a desk drawer.

"Hello, I would like to speak to Elaine. Thank you." While he waited for Elaine to come to the phone, he pulled a pencil out of the drawer. Noticing there was no scratch pad, he closed the drawer.

"Hello, Elaine. I'm sorry I couldn't make it for our tennis game this morning. But I'll make it up to you. Instead of me coming there and we go out to eat, how about you driving over to Monrose and we'll have supper on the porch?

Later we could walk along the beach or dance here at the house. Alone. Just the two of us."

The voice on the other end of the phone softened.

"Casual," said Elliot. "That's great! Am I forgiven? Great! I'll see you around seven."

While he was talking, he pulled the piece of paper a little way out from under the blotter and made some circles and x's on it. After he hung up the phone, Elliot pulled it out from under the blotter. It was an envelope. Thinking Alice may not have seen it while cleaning, he left it out on top of the desk so she could put it away.

Elliot headed for the kitchen to check out the food. If he needed anything extra, he would send Ernie for it.

Elaine arrived around seven o'clock. Elliot answered the door since Alice had left an hour earlier to join a friend for supper and the movies. Ernie told Elliot earlier that he was going bowling with his team tonight. Since they were in a tournament, it would be late when he would return home. *Perfect,* thought Elliot. He and Elaine had the mansion to themselves for a while. He admired Elaine's soft pink dress, thinking how easy it would be to slip it off her. Elaine, taking Elliot by the arm, broke into his thoughts.

It was about two in the morning when Elliot kissed Elaine, as she sat in her red Chevy convertible, bending down and smelling the sweet scent of her body as he did so. He watched the car lights go through the gates and turn as she headed down the main road by the ocean. *A wonderful evening,* he thought, *but I didn't get her in bed. The next time though . . .*

Elliot closed the front door and locked it. In the living room, he looked over the collection before he turned the lights out. Then he went into the library through the double doors from the living room, turning off the two lamps there. He came out into the hall and checked the french doors at the rear and proceeded down the side hall into the study.

Reaching to turn the light off on the desk, he noticed the envelope on which he had doodled. Elliot started to put it away in the desk when a sudden urge came over him to open it and read the contents.

Pulling out two documents, Elliot looked at the one with the border. He sat down in the desk chair reading the document. It was a copy of a birth certificate with his uncle's name and a woman's name that he didn't recognize. The name of the child listed on the certificate was Sarah Anne. The birth date listed on the certificate was that of Sarah, his cousin. A low, drawn-out sigh came from Elliot as he grasped the significance of what he was holding.

Sarah was Uncle Bill's child out of wedlock. *She is Uncle Bill's heir,* thought Elliot. Evidently, Sarah didn't know it. *That was why Uncle Bill left her an interest in the business.*

His Uncle Dan and Aunt Jennifer had raised her as their own. Elliot wondered if his mother knew about Uncle Bill and Sarah. Well, he'd call her later this morning. Right now, the secret seemed to be safe. He was tired. Turning off the light, Elliot took the envelope with him. When he got to his room upstairs, he put it in a safe place, took a shower, and went to bed. Sleep came quickly.

———

Elliot didn't hear anyone when he came down the backstairs. It was very quiet. He heard noises from the kitchen as he approached the door. As he came through the swinging door, he saw Alice putting away the dishes.

"Good morning," he said. "I guess I'm late for breakfast."

"Yes. We ate about three hours ago. It's about time for lunch."

"Who ate with you?" Elliot inquired.

"Ernie came over, telling about last night. His team won first place. He's one happy guy. Said that his team now competes with the first-place team of the Bowl Away Competition. His team won a hefty cash prize for last night's win."

"Well, more power to him. I could never get interested in bowling. Tennis is my game," said Elliot. "You don't have to fix me anything to eat. I'll take care of my breakfast, if you don't mind."

"No, help yourself. I need to get ready for church."

Elliot looked around for the Sunday paper.

"Have you seen the paper?"

"Ernie was reading it while he was eating breakfast. If it isn't on the table, he probably took it with him. He'll bring it back this afternoon," replied Alice.

"That's OK," responded Elliot. He'd read the paper over at his mother's this afternoon.

When Alice left the kitchen, Elliot went to work preparing his meal, more like lunch than breakfast.

About an hour later, he called his mother.

"Hello, Mother. Are you going to be in this afternoon?"

"Yes, dear," she replied.

"I'd like to come over if you're not busy."

"I would love to see you. It's been awhile," his mother commented.

"OK, I'll see you in about an hour," he said, then hung up the phone.

Elliot locked up the mansion, put his duffel bag in the car and drove unhurriedly along the ocean, thinking about how he could ask what he wanted to know without letting his mother know what he found out about Uncle Bill and Sarah's relationship. Maybe his mother knew but wouldn't tell him. He'd just have to feel her out.

Chapter 14

The sun warmed the room where Elliot sat on a sofa. His mother's voice drifted from the next room where she was talking on the phone. Elliot always enjoyed this room. It was a place of security to him. He would sit in this room as a little boy when he had bad days at school or just felt lonely. The room was cheerful, with a wall full of windows through which the sun beamed on the ferns, philodendron, and violets sitting on tables in front of the windows. Outside the windows was the old chestnut tree. He and Sarah spent many a summer day climbing its branches. *It was good to be in this room again.* He needed security now. The room made him feel a lot better.

"I hope we don't have any more interruptions, dear. Janice has been away for two weeks and wanted to catch up on what was going on in the clubs we both belong to," his mother explained as she entered the room. "She has just returned from London where she visited with her husband. He'll be moving with his office to Rome next month. She said she plans to join him there in two months. They plan to rent their house here. If you know of anyone looking to rent a home, let her know. It'll be for ten months, though, instead of a year."

"I'll keep that in mind," said Elliot. "Talking of people being away, have you heard anything from Sarah? I was looking at the chestnut tree while you were on the phone and thought about the summers Sarah and I played in that old tree."

"Goodness, that was some time ago."

Pause. "Did Uncle Bill ever have any girlfriends?"

"Why do you ask?" his mother replied.

"Well, Uncle Bill was a handsome man and I just wondered if he ever had a girlfriend. He never dated anyone that I knew of during the years I worked with him."

"Now that you asked, yes he did. It was a long time ago. They went steady in high school and college. They had planned to marry a year after they graduated. Bill went to work at the company. I guess he'd been working there for a year when they split up. In fact, it was about three months before their wedding. I don't know exactly what happened because I was busy with you and your dad.

"You were about a month old when Bill came to visit and told us Margaret had gone to live with an aunt in Ohio for a while. He was upset. He loved her very much and was having a hard time realizing that he and Margaret would never be married. Your dad and I did what we could to comfort him. He never did tell us what had led to the breakup."

"Did Uncle Bill ever see Margaret again?" Margaret was the name of the woman on Sarah's birth certificate.

"Well, surprisingly, Margaret visited with us about a year later. She said she had stopped by Bill's place but he was out. We invited her to stay for dinner and she did. Margaret thanked us for being so kind to her. I knew she wasn't sure what kind of reception she would receive. We were finishing up dinner when Bill arrived. He said his housekeeper told him Margaret had stopped by and had gone over to his sister's house. He and Margaret left together. After that night, Bill never spoke of her again," said his mother.

"Did Uncle Dan and Aunt Jennifer know what happened?"

"They knew just about as much as your father and I did." Anne paused and wondered if she should tell Elliot the truth about Sarah. Would he keep quiet? *I should share the secret with someone. It might as well be my son,* Anne reflected. *Secrets like this should be kept in the family and not told to strangers.*

"Well, I'll tell you a secret about Sarah which only a few family members know. Sarah doesn't know what I'm going to tell you, so please don't go telling her. Someday she may know." *I hope I am doing the right thing,* Anne thought to herself. "Sarah is adopted."

"Sarah's adopted?" Elliot echoed, pretending surprise. "When was she adopted? I've known her all my life."

"Oh, let's see now. I guess you were about a year old. Dan and Jennifer were very excited about getting Sarah. I remember Bill was very happy they had adopted a baby. He spent as much time as he could with them. The company was growing and taking more of his time. Now, please dear, don't say anything to Sarah."

"No, no I won't," said Elliot. "I'll keep the secret."

"Why didn't Uncle Dan and Aunt Jennifer tell Sarah?" Elliot inquired.

"Oh, they were going to. They planned to tell her when she was ten but decided that maybe she was too young. So they decided they would tell her when she was twelve. They thought she would be mature enough to understand at that age. Well, her twelfth year came and went. Sarah was very happy, and Dan and Jennifer weren't sure how she would receive the news. It went on like this until she went away to college. By then they had decided to leave things alone. They would tell her someday, they said, but not now.

"The car crash ended their debate about when to tell Sarah. Sarah may never know now unless you or I tell her. As far as I know, we're the only ones who know about Sarah's adoption," his mother concluded.

"Well, her mother knows." A pause. "I wonder if she's still alive."

"I've never thought about that. You're right," his mother said. "I wonder where she is."

A few minutes passed in silence as each contemplated the possibility of Sarah's mother being alive . . . somewhere.

Then Elliot broke the silence. "That is a surprising story about Uncle Bill . . . and Sarah. What else do you know about the family that you're keeping secret?" Elliot teased his mother. "Hey, am I adopted?" he asked smiling.

"No, you silly dear. Your dad and I would have told you. We're not like your Uncle Dan and Aunt Jennifer. It's the child's right to know they're adopted. I've thought about telling Sarah since her parents' death. But, my dear, it's not my place. However, if Sarah ever asked me, I'd tell her. I don't know why she would, though. As far as I know, she believes Uncle Dan and Aunt Jennifer were her true parents."

Leaving Wellesley and his childhood home behind him, Elliot drove down Route 9 toward the tennis club. Elliot's mission was successful. *Well,* he thought to himself, *Uncle Bill is Sarah's father, and Margaret's last visit to Uncle Bill was to let him know about the baby. That was probably why she went away.* He wondered why they never married, and if Uncle Dan and Aunt Jennifer knew Sarah was Uncle Bill's child. Mother didn't say. He wondered if Mother knew. *Well, I think she would have told me if she knew,* he reasoned.

Driving without paying attention to the traffic or the road, the thought that Sarah was Uncle Bill's true heir bothered Elliot. They were not equal anymore—not a nephew and a niece to Uncle Bill, but a nephew and a daughter. Cold chills traveled down his spine.

What would happen to his inheritance if it was known that Sarah was the real heir? Would Sarah claim the inheritance? Would she kick him out of the business? Yes, the thought bothered Elliot deeply. His only consolation was that right now, no one else knew what he did.

Many of the members had left the court by the time Elliot arrived at the club. It was late. Some were sitting on the terrace overlooking the courts, drinking their favorite drinks while others had gone inside to get ready for the evening meal. He didn't see Elaine on the terrace so he went into the clubhouse lobby to look around, and then into the library.

As he approached a table in the center of the room, Elliot noticed the Sunday paper was opened to the local section. Elliot stood and looked at the photo and the headline above it, "Prominent Boston Antique Dealer Killed in Crash." He couldn't believe it. He grabbed the paper and sat in a nearby chair, reading the story. Elliot became pale. The import of the article hit him. He felt despair closing in around him. He cannot afford to panic. If he did, he wouldn't be able to think clearly. He had to think about what to do now. He couldn't lose control right now.

Elliot forgot Elaine, forgot about supper at the club, forgot where he was. The front desk clerk roused Elliot from his thoughts about two hours after he entered the club's library. The clerk was closing it and the study area for the night.

Elliot asked him if Elaine had left. The clerk, a young college student who worked there for about two years now, knew the members by name and the gossip about most of them. He informed Elliot she had left with a couple she'd been playing tennis with. *I'll call her later,* thought Elliot.

He thanked the clerk and slowly lifted himself from the chair. Exhaustion was creeping through his body as he went across the porch, down the steps, and across the parking lot to his car. Elliot's panic eased and he was thinking a little more clearly. *Well, I can't do anything right now,* he thought. *I'll have to find someone else to buy the collection. It's Sunday night. Probably can't find anyone tonight.*

Elliot thought about the day's events as he drove to his condo across from the Boston Gardens—his discovery of Sarah's true parents and the death of Mr. Jewel. He showered when he got home. The hot water was relaxing.

The clock on the mantel chimed ten thirty when Elliot entered the living room. He poured himself a bourbon. This was his third call to Elaine and his third drink. The phone on the other end was ringing. He had left two messages already. He started to speak when it dawned on him that he was listening to Elaine's recorded message. *Still out,* he thought.

Elliot looked in the yellow pages under "Antiques." He scanned the several pages of antique dealers. A shop in Essex caught his eye. He called, hoping they may have an answering machine. A sleepy female voice answered after several rings. It took a few seconds for Elliot to apprehend that the voice belonged to a live person—it was not a recorded message.

He briefly told her what he had to sell. She seemed interested and made an appointment to see the collection at ten in the morning.

Sighing as he hung up the phone, Elliot sat down on the sofa. He was tired and so he lay down. Just for a few minutes, he told himself as his eyelids closed.

Chapter 15

Sarah tingled with excitement. Jason was just as curious as she was about the will change. From what Mr. Abbot said, it seemed she may be favored with more of Uncle Bill's estate. But why would Uncle Bill change his will? She knew he and Elliot didn't get along from time to time. They had their disagreements, but then they would patch things up between them. *I wonder what Elliot did that made Uncle Bill so mad he would change his will?*

I shouldn't sit around "supposing" why Uncle Bill changed his will. We may never know. I should be getting to bed, but I'm not yet sleepy. I'll take a walk around the complex, thought Sarah.

She slipped into her shoes, ran the brush through her hair, and searched through her purse for the apartment key. Retrieving it from the bottom, Sarah put it into the pocket of her slacks.

The air was warm. A breeze blew Sarah's hair into her face. She stood outside her apartment building for a few minutes looking up at the sky, picking out the Big Dipper, the North Star, and a few other familiar constellations. The complex was quiet tonight. Most of the lights were off in the buildings that she passed. Tomorrow was Monday, a workday for most people. *Well,* she thought, *I'll be back in the workforce soon.* Sarah couldn't believe that the average length of time to find a job was eight months. Several articles she read recently told job searchers to expect the search to take that long. *I'm sure I can find a good job in three months.*

Sarah came around a curve as a van headed toward her. It was picking up speed as it got closer. *They're going too fast to make the curve,* Sarah thought. She stood on the side of the street next to several cars parked vertically, praying the van would slow down. It didn't. She was in the van's full lights. *It's coming right at me!* Sarah stepped between the parked cars and then instinctively began running for the lawn. The van hit the car next to her, and she felt something heavy hit her thigh. She stumbled and fell onto the lawn in front of the parked cars.

Not moving, Sarah lay on the lawn for a few minutes listening as the van skidded around the curve and sped up the hill. As she was raising herself up off the ground, Sarah felt a pair of strong hands under her arms guiding her upward and someone asking, "Are you all right? That sure was a close call."

A woman with a German shepherd came running over to her. "That driver was crazy. I was walking Buster, and that van came speeding up behind me. It sure scared Buster. Are you OK?" she asked.

"I'm fine. Thank you both for helping me. I think all I have are bruises. You said it was a van?"

Both of her helpers said yes.

"Could you see what color it was?"

"It was a dark color," said the woman. "It looked red under the streetlights. I'm going to tell management about this. You could've been killed."

The man was looking at one of the cars. "This one was hit by the van. The taillight is knocked out, and the trunk has been dented. The impact moved it a little ways. The car next to it looks OK. At least in this streetlight," he said.

"I'll go into the building here to see who owns this car," he said as he wrote down the license number.

Sarah and the woman waited for him.

A few minutes later, the man appeared with a woman whose hair was in curlers and was wearing a house robe. He introduced her as Marsha Duncan. She examined the car, upset about the damage. She asked them if they would tell the police what happened because she was going to call them. They said they would and gave her their names and apartment numbers.

"Do you want me to walk you to your apartment?" the man asked Sarah.

"You both have been so kind, why don't both of you join me for coffee? We can call the office's answering service and tell them what happened tonight," Sarah suggested.

"Well, thank you," said the man. "I'll be glad to join you."

"By the way, my name is Brown Shawn."

"And I'm Lois Cloverpart."

And turning to Lois, Sarah asked, "Will you be joining us?"

"Yes," she said, and they went with Sarah to her apartment.

Ginger stayed under the bed all the time they visited. Sarah noticed Buster was a well-behaved dog. He looked like a small German shepherd, only that he had long floppy ears and a long tail that curled over his back. They called the office's answering service and reported the incident. It was late when Sarah's new friends left for their apartments.

Chapter 16

There was unusual activity for a Monday morning in the accounting department manager's office at Crosswood Enterprises, one of Monrose Industries' entities. It was seven o'clock, and the manager was sitting with several of her accountants looking at a monitor. One of the accountants was pointing to an entry on the screen and was talking about it. The manager closed the door to the office as more employees came in to work. An hour later, the accountants left the office, and the manager called Elliot Winter's office.

"No, Mr. Winter is not in. He won't be in this morning," the secretary said. "He does plan to be in the office this afternoon."

"This can't wait until this afternoon. Tell him to call me now. It's urgent," Sylvia Williams advised. "There is a problem, and he needs to know about it."

"I'll page him," said Winter's secretary. "Can you tell me what the problem is?"

"Not right now. It's best if Mr. Winter hears it from me first so that he can decide how he wants to handle it. It's imperative that he calls me. I would appreciate it if you reach him as quickly as possible."

"I'll do that," she said.

"Thank you," responded Mrs. Williams.

Several of the staff worked over the weekend to bring accounts up-to-date. One of the accountants, Fred, discovered an unusual entry in an account which he had accessed by accident, an account which didn't have much activity. He called on several of his coworkers to verify what he had discovered and then started looking at some other accounts. They found four accounts tampered with. Fred had stumbled on a skimming operation. There appeared to be a lot of money missing, and he and his coworkers did not find the money transferred to other accounts. It was gone.

Sylvia didn't want to alarm any of the employees or stockholders, so she instructed those who discovered the problem to remain quiet until Mr. Winter made a decision on how to handle it. Right now, the lid had to be kept on it.

Sylvia and her staff had never seen anything like it. It was cleverly concealed, and if Fred hadn't accidentally accessed the wrong account, it would never have been discovered. Because of the way it was done, they all knew it had to be someone in the company, someone familiar with the account structure and good with computers. They all knew they have to keep quiet about it for a little longer. Meanwhile, they took turns monitoring the activity in the system. Maybe the thief would access that account again.

Chapter 17

Alice had coffee and danish ready for Elliot and his guest. She had planned to go shopping this morning and was on the way out of the house when Elliot called her. He informed her he would be there around 9:30, and a guest would arrive a little later. He requested coffee and danish and explained the guest as a potential business partner.

Alice was shocked when she read about the death of Mr. Jewel. She recalled the conversation she had with him on Saturday. He seemed very taken with the house and its contents.

Elliot was on time. Thirty minutes later, a tall, large woman with sandy hair in her late thirties arrived in a brown panel van. She introduced herself as Arlene Dire. Alice let her in and showed her into the study where Elliot had asked Alice to set up the coffee.

"Thank you, Alice," Elliot said and nodded his head to dismiss her.

Alice returned to the kitchen. She was full of curiosity. She wanted to listen at the study door but decided it would be best to keep her curiosity in check for it might get her into trouble. *There are some things that are best not to know of,* Alice thought. *It's best to keep my nose out of this.* She poured herself a cup of coffee, took a danish, and sat down at the kitchen table and began reading the mystery of the month from her book club.

"Hello. I'm Elliot Winter. I'm so glad you were able to come over on short notice, Mrs. Dire."

"Well, my ten o'clock appointment had called about an hour before you did last night and canceled. You were in luck," she replied. "What is it that you have to offer me?"

"Coffee?" offered Elliot.

"You have coffee to sell?" asked an astonished Mrs. Dire.

"Oh, no!" replied Elliot, surprised. "I mean, do you want a cup of coffee before we proceed with our discussion?"

"Yes, thank you."

While Elliot poured the coffee, Mrs. Dire looked around the room. Taking the filled cup and saucer from Elliot, she asked, "Now, what is it you want to sell? You must want me to like it a lot, or you would not have gone to the trouble of serving coffee and danish."

"You're right." Elliot smiled. "I don't serve refreshments to everyone who visits here."

"Well then, show me what you have."

"I do have a nice collection, which the late Mr. Jewel was going to buy. As you know, he died in a wreck Saturday, and we never closed the deal officially. I think you'll find it a good collection. It belonged to my uncle, Bill Monrose. When he died, he left the estate and its contents to me."

"You have my condolences," Mrs. Dire replied.

"Thank you," murmured Elliot.

"Tell me, what kind of a collection is this? Books, china, silver, paintings?"

"Well, it does contain a few old books, jewelry, Chinese vases, and other fine collectibles," replied Elliot.

"I deal mainly with furniture, paintings, old rugs, and china."

"This is a very special collection which my uncle gathered from around the world through his travels. The books are first editions."

"I'll take a look." Mrs. Dire finished her danish and coffee.

Elliot then took her to the living room to the cases containing the collection. He pointed out the Chinese vases to Mrs. Dire. She seemed delighted with them.

"I like the vases. I may have a few buyers for them. But I have no use for the other items. They are good, mind you, but the clients I do business with are not interested in books or jewelry."

Elliot sighed. "Are you sure your clients wouldn't be interested in the books?"

"Well, I know a collector who also sometimes sells antiques. He may be interested. I'll give him a call and ask him if he'd like to see what you have here," said Mrs. Dire.

Elliot looked distressed.

"I'm sorry. I see you are disappointed. Don't worry, I'll keep my eyes and ears open to those who express an interest in what you have," said Mrs. Dire.

"I'm disappointed. Mr. Jewel said it was an excellent collection," said Elliot.

"It is. But I don't have the type of clients Mr. Jewel had. Mr. Jewel dabbled in everything of any worth. I only dabble in particular antiques. Can I bring clients over to look at the vases?" Mrs. Dire asked.

"Yes, you may. Do you think this collector will want to purchase the rest of these items?"

"I don't know. I'll call him when I get back to the shop. If he's interested, he'll call you today. How's that?"

"Well," said Elliot, "that will have to do."

Elliot escorted Mrs. Dire to the front door. She held out her hand and Elliot grasped it, shaking it. "I would appreciate that."

"Thank you for the coffee, Mr. Winter. I'll call you about the vases."

He closed the door and through the side door panes, watched her drive out to the main road.

Elliot discerned he may not be able to sell the collection as quickly as he thought. *I have till Saturday to get the money together.* Nothing liquid. It was all tied up in the business or an investment where it would take more than a week to access. He was wondering why Henry had to have the money now when Ernie walked into the room.

"Mr. Elliot, I brought your pager in from the car. It was beeping as I walked by," Ernie explained. "I thought it might be important."

"Thank you." Looking at the pager, he said, "It's the office. Probably wondering when I'll be in today."

Ernie went down the hall and disappeared into the corridor leading into the kitchen. Alice was taking up the coffee and dishes when Elliot looked into the study. "Anything else I can do for you before I go out?"

"No, no. Thank you for setting up the coffee," Elliot said distracted.

Elliot paced around the study while Alice finished putting all the dishes on the tray. When she left, Elliot was looking out a window through which the garden could be seen. It was full of red, pink, yellow, and white blossoms. But Elliot didn't see them. He paced slowly to the other window, looking over the ocean.

He loved this place, and he didn't want to lose it. He paced back to the other window. Mrs. Dire didn't give Elliot much hope of selling all the collection by Saturday. The phone rang, but Elliot thought Alice would answer it. It rang a few more times. Then he remembered she left to go shopping. He hurried to the desk and picked up the phone.

"I was getting ready to hang up," the voice on the other end said. "May I speak with Mr. Elliot Winter?"

"This is he."

"I understand you have a valuable collection you wish to sell."

"Who did you hear that from?"

"Mrs. Dire of Essex Isle Antiques. She called just a few minutes ago and described some of the items. I have a client who is interested."

"She certainly works fast."

"My client is here with me. He has a few questions to ask."

"All right, put him on."

A pause, then, "You're getting desperate to part with some of your uncle's collection." Elliot recognized the voice. It was Henry.

"I didn't know you were into antiques."

"I dabble a bit from time to time. When Carl told me who the seller was, I had to give you a call. I could help you out and buy them. Or I could let you sweat it out."

"Mrs. Dire has other clients who might be interested," replied Elliot.

"I instructed Carl to tell her not to call anyone else about buying the collection."

"You what?"

"You deal with me and only me."

"What are you going to do? Are you going to buy them?" Elliot was irritated.

"I'm going to think on it. It certainly is a small world, eh, Elliot?" said Henry, laughing as he hung up the phone.

It certainly is, thought Elliot.

Chapter 18

It was around ten o'clock when Sarah finished up the breakfast dishes. She had just turned on the dishwasher when the phone rang.

"Hello, Sarah."

"Good morning, Mrs. Greyson. I guess you heard about the speeding van from last night."

"I certainly have," replied Mrs. Greyson. "Veny said he's checking out what happened. He said he'll drop by this morning and get some details of last night's incident. From what I heard, it sounds as if the driver was high on drugs, or he was aiming to run over you."

"Well, when I found out the van was probably red, the thought that it could have been the same van I saw the other evening occurred to me. And later, I have to admit, the thought that the van was trying to run me down did occur to me too. If that's the case, then those guys saw me on the porch."

"Well, my dear, you do need my Veny's help."

Sarah had no sooner hung up the phone when Veny was ringing the doorbell.

After he left, Sarah called Jason. She didn't want to call him at the office, but Sarah didn't want to wait any longer to share with him what happened last night.

"Hi, Jason! Are you busy?"

"Hi, honey. No, I was just thinking about you."

"Well, I have something to share with you, and it may take some time," Sarah explained.

"I've got the time for you, sweetheart, always will. Let me tell Betty to hold all my calls."

Jason returned a few minutes later, closing the door to his office.

"OK. We're all alone," Jason said.

Sarah told him about the events of last night's close encounter with the van and what she, Mrs. Greyson, and Veny thought was behind it.

"Oh, my dear Sarah," he sighed. "I had a feeling that something bad was happening over the past several days. Now you confirm it. I'll be out there Friday instead of Saturday. I wish I could get there sooner. I'll make the change as soon as we hang up. Don't protest now."

"I am. It's not necessary," Sarah stated. "One day doesn't make any difference. The police are checking into it, and Veny says a policeman will be driving by here every two hours."

"That's good, but I should be with you. Wish I was there now. I'll call you in a little while to give you the new arrival time. Please be careful, honey."

"I will be, sweet man," replied Sarah.

Chapter 19

Elliot was pulling into the company's parking lot when his pager went off again. He had been paged twice on his way there, but he didn't bother to call the office. He'd be there soon enough. This Monday was not getting off to a good start.

Wilma, his secretary, gave him the phone messages as he passed through the outer office. She followed him into his office.

"As you see from the messages, Mrs. Williams has been calling you with some urgency. She wants you to call her. She won't tell me what she wants to talk to you about."

"Thank you. I'll call Mrs. Williams. Is there anything else I should know about?"

"No, sir," Wilma responded. "Is there anything you want me to take care of?"

"Not right now. Please close the door as you leave." Wilma left his office, closing the door after her.

Elliot wasn't sure if he wanted to talk to Mrs. Williams. He suspected the shortage he created may have been found. But, then again, it could be something else. *What else could be so urgent?* He could put off calling her, but he needed to know. With trepidation, he picked up the phone and punched in her extension.

"This is Mrs. Williams."

"This is Elliot Winter returning your call," he spoke in a clear, calm voice.

"Thank you for returning my call, Mr. Winter. We have a problem, which you should know about. Can you come to my office so that I can explain to you what we've found? This afternoon? It does need your immediate attention."

"Can you tell me what it is?" he asked, keeping anxiety out of his voice.

"No, not over the phone. It's best that you see for yourself."

"OK. I'll be there shortly." Elliot dreaded talking to Mrs. Williams. *She probably knows. I'm going to have to put on a good face—be my charming, confident self.*

Sylvia had the door opened to her office. Elliot walked past two offices before approaching her door. He paused in the doorway before he said hello. The jade suit she wore was a striking contrast to her ebony skin. She was attractive, and the jade suit magnified her physical beauty. Sylvia, who was standing at the file cabinet, didn't see him in the doorway and jumped when Elliot said hello.

"Oh, hello, Mr. Winter. Sorry I jumped like that. I'm just nervous about what we found this weekend," said Sylvia. "I'm glad you're here. Let me call Fred. He's the one who found money missing. Lots of it."

"Oh no," Elliot said aloud, wondering what was going to happen next. *Just keep cool,* he told himself.

Sylvia called Fred who was at the door within minutes.

"Hello, Fred. Mr. Winter, this is Fred Greene."

"Hello, Fred."

"Fred, this is Mr. Winter."

"Hello, sir."

"Fred was working here this weekend when he stumbled across money being missing. Fred, please tell Mr. Winter how you found it and how much is missing."

Before Fred said anything, Elliot knew what they discovered. Right now, no one suspected him. He had to keep it that way.

Fred repeated his story to Elliot and showed him on the computer the accounts affected by the embezzlement. Elliot pretended he didn't know the specific workings of the accounting system and asked questions. He asked if they suspected anyone, and her reply was no. Sylvia told him they were monitoring the system for any unusual activity.

After Fred left, Sylvia informed Elliot she had alerted the security department. "If we had the finance security module running that Mr. Monrose had installed, we would've been alerted sooner and probably caught whoever did it," said Sylvia. "Too bad it had all those bugs."

"You're probably right. But you did the right thing. I apologize for not calling you sooner. I didn't realize the immensity of the problem. And you're right not to share this with anyone else right now. It's best to keep it quiet. Please make sure that Fred and the other staff say nothing about this to anyone. Ha, ha, not even to their pets," Elliot laughed, attempting to ease the seriousness of the situation.

"I just hope the press doesn't get wind of this," Elliot continued. "We don't need negative publicity so soon after Uncle Bill's uh, Mr. Monrose's death." He turned to leave and then paused at the door. Facing Mrs. Williams, he said,

"Well, again, thank you. And keep me posted. I would like to know who is doing this. Uh, by the way, that suit looks great on you."

"Well . . . thank you, sir," responded Mrs. Williams, taken off guard.

Elliot returned to his office. He wondered how he was going to fix the accounts next week to make it look like money was deposited. He'd worry about that next week. Right now, he has to get the rest of the money Henry was demanding. He picked up the phone book and flipped through the yellow pages until he found the heading "Antique Dealers." He scanned down the column and found a dealer who might help him out and punched in the number.

Chapter 20

Alice went to the TV set in her room to pick up the TV schedule when the phone rang. It was about time for the Monday afternoon mystery hour to start. Alice debated a few seconds whether to answer the phone because she didn't want to miss any of the program. The ringing phone won and she rushed over to answer it.

"Hello," she said, "this is Alice Sherry."

"Hello, Alice," said Larry. "Are you busy right now?"

"Oh no."

"Good. I'm calling in reference to the documents you told me were missing when you went to put them away this morning. I remember you said that Elliot was there this weekend."

"Right," replied Alice.

"I think Elliot has those documents. And I think one is a copy of Bill's codicil to his will. Bill wrote it the day before he died."

"A codicil?" replied Alice, puzzled.

"Yes. It showed up here several days ago. It changes the heir to his estate and business."

"Oh my," uttered Alice.

"If Elliot has a copy of the codicil, then he knows who the heir is. The rightful heir," said Larry.

"Who is the heir?" she inquired.

"I'll tell you as soon as I tell the new heir. And I'll be talking to her Monday."

"I'll have to wait that long to find out? I don't know if my curiosity can stand it."

Larry chuckled. "You'll live. You'll make it through Monday. Would you let me know if Elliot shows up? Keep an eye on him. Let me know if he tries to sell anything or move anything out of the house."

"Oh my. Do you think he would do that?"

"I don't know," replied Larry.

"Humm. I just recalled he had several antique dealers here. He took them to the living room. Ooohh, do you think he may have already sold some things? Like Mr. Bill's collection?"

"Thank you for telling me. I'll get some paperwork started to keep Elliot from selling anything. Don't let him know we had this conversation," Larry warned Alice. "But let Ernie know."

"OK, I won't say a word to Elliot. And I'll tell Ernie."

"By the way, yours and Ernie's inheritances are not affected by the change."

"Oh, that is good news," replied Alice.

Larry concluded his conversation and hung up the phone.

So Elliot already plans to sell some of the estate. *I wonder what kind of trouble he's in,* thought Larry.

Chapter 21

Elliot's last client of the day had left when his secretary beeped him on the intercom.

"Mr. Winter, I have a call for you from Mr. Abbot. Do you wish to take it?" A brief pause followed. Elliot really didn't want to talk to him. The attorney had left him several messages on his home phone answering machine Friday night. Could it be that he knew about Sarah's birth? Is that what this call is about?

"Mr. Winter, do you want to talk to Mr. Abbot? He's holding."

"OK. Put him on," Elliot sighed, knowing he didn't want to hear what Mr. Abbot had to say.

"Hello, Larry, What can I do for you?"

"You can be at my office next Monday afternoon at four o'clock," responded Larry.

"Why?"

"A codicil to your Uncle's will was found recently. It supersedes a section of his previous will and it will be read at that time." A long pause.

"Hello, are you there?" asked Larry.

"Yes, yes. I'm surprised to learn about this codicil. Can you tell me the contents?"

"I won't go into details now. However, don't sell or spend anything you have inherited from your uncle."

"Am I losing some of the inheritance?"

"Yes," replied Larry.

"How much?"

"You'll find out by Monday. Be at my office at four o'clock," Larry told him.

"OK, I'll be there," Elliot replied with reluctance.

Elliot hung up the phone in disbelief.

"It can't be. It just can't be. She's going to get it after all," Elliot said aloud. *Damn her. She's not interested in the business. There must be a way to discredit her claim. Everything is mine until Sarah is notified. I'll sell what I want. I thought Bill wouldn't have had the time to change his will. Apparently he did. This whole day is turning out bad.*

Elliot thumbed through his Rolodex and came to a card. Picking up the phone, he called the number listed on it.

After a few rings, a woman's voice responded, "Attorney for All Reasons."

"Is Wally in?" he inquired.

Chapter 22

Sarah began to settle down from the events of the last twenty-four hours. She was hungry, and the clock on the end table says it was close to six. Sarah fed Ginger earlier, and now the cat was curled up on the bed, asleep.

The apartment was shady, now that the sun was making its descent in the western sky. The shadow of her apartment building was getting longer on the parking lot pavement. Sarah needed to pick up the mail, so she decided to eat out. She grabbed her purse from the bedroom nightstand, drove to the mailboxes, then headed for the Vickery at the old Roswell mill. She thought about calling Mrs. Greyson to invite her to go with her but decided not to. She really wanted to be alone right now.

Sarah felt secure since Jason was arriving on Friday. His flight was landing the same time it would have on Saturday. She didn't want Jason to worry. Sarah thought about what he said regarding his foreboding and hoped he felt better about the situation. At least Jason seemed to be in better spirits when he called to tell her about his flight changes.

Being in the old mill perked her up. Pushing last night's events out of her mind, she stopped and parked at Roswell's Historic Square. She strolled around the square, observing the old buildings clustered around it. A large white-framed gazebo stood in the middle of the green square surrounded by crepe myrtles and hardwoods. Sarah sat on a bench and watched tourists visit the boutiques and shops. It was near closing time and a few tourists hurried to another shop before it closed. When the sun disappeared over the hill, Sarah left the bench—it was time to go home.

Traveling down Holcomb Bridge Road, Sarah looked in her rearview mirror. A red van was two cars behind her. She turned into Thoroughbred Acres frequently looking through the rearview mirror. The van turned and followed her. Sarah could feel fear pushing its way into her thought. *There was no need to submit to it. The police were patrolling the apartment complex.* She went around the circle and turned onto the road that leads to the section were she lived. Sarah slowed down and watched through the rearview mirror for the red van. The van drove past her road and turned onto the second road. Sarah sighed in relief. *I'm still jumpy,* she thought.

Chapter 23

Elliot delighted in the view from his Boylston condominium, eight stories above Boston Garden. The day had started off better than yesterday. His spirits lifted since he had found several antique dealers willing to take the collection off his hands. But they couldn't guarantee that the cash would be ready for him by Saturday morning. They told him they would let him know by late Thursday. Elliot liked to play it close but this was a little too close.

He heard nothing from Sylvia about the embezzlement since they talked yesterday. Elliot picked up the phone and keyed in Sylvia's office number.

"Hello, is this Sylvia?"

"Yes."

"This is Winter. Anything new on the missing money?"

"No sir," replied Sylvia. "It has been very quiet."

"Hum. They've probably taken all they want and have long gone. But please continue with the monitoring," Elliot told Sylvia. "And keep me posted."

"Have you notified the authorities or alerted the board?"

"No I haven't. Company security is conducting the investigation. When they find the culprits, we'll let the authorities know and turn the culprits over to them. I'll let the board know in due time."

If he told her any different, Sylvia would be suspicious. He called Wilma to let her know he would be late for his first appointment.

"Please tell them to wait and extend my apologies to each one," said Elliot.

His calendar was full with meetings today.

Chapter 24

Sarah thought she did well on her interview with Bob Lewis. But this was her first job interview, and she didn't have anything to compare it with, except what she had read in the books on job interviews. He asked only a few questions the books listed that could be asked in an interview. Bob exclaimed several times what a small world it was when he found that Sarah knew Larry Abbot. He ended up talking about his law-school days where he met Larry.

Everyone has their own way of doing things, thought Sarah. He said he would let her know his decision next week. She was not at all enthused about the position. *But the building and grounds were sure nice.*

The tall building, about twenty floors, was surrounded by acres of beautiful landscaped lawns. In the back, a two-level terrace looked over a small lake fed by a stream. The lake was stocked with fish, which swam close to the terrace. Sarah leaned over the wall to watch them move just below the surface of the water. It was a delightful setting. Sarah fell in love with the spot.

Even though she might not get the job, she was elated to have the interview. That meant the resume and cover letter were working. *That's great!*

Sarah was starting her exit from GA 400 onto Holcomb Bridge when she looked into her rearview mirror.

My gosh! That sure looks like the red van. Well, I am not going to panic. Let's see now, what can I do? Or should I do anything?

Sarah moved onto Holcomb Bridge Road and watched through her rearview mirror for the red van. It was three cars behind her. Sarah needed to pick up groceries. *I'm not going to let them intimidate me. I'll stop at the grocery store.* She pulled into the store lot and parked close to the store's entrance. She sat in the Corolla for a few minutes, looking for the van. Not seeing it, Sarah went into the store thinking, *They're not going to bully me.*

She felt safe in the grocery and took her time shopping. When she was ready to leave, Sarah stood at the store's large window for a few minutes looking for the red van. She didn't see it, so she pushed her cart full of groceries to her car and loaded them into the backseat.

Looking out the rearview mirror every few minutes, Sarah made her way down Holcomb Bridge Road to Thoroughbred Acres. She didn't see the red van until she turned into the apartment complex. It was right behind her. Sarah speeded up and the van kept up with her. Then Sarah got an idea. She pulled into the office's parking lot and went into the office. The van went on by.

"Hi, Pam. May I use your phone for a few minutes?" Sarah inquired.

"Of course, Mrs. Edmonds," she replied.

Sarah keyed in the number and the phone rang twice.

"Mrs. Greyson, I'm so glad you're home. The red van is following me. I'm calling from the office here at the apartment complex. I was wondering if you could meet me outside my apartment? I think they won't do anything if they see someone else with me."

"I sure will," replied Mrs. Greyson. "Start out now and I'll be waiting on the sidewalk in front of your building."

"Thank you so much."

Mrs. Greyson met Sarah and helped her into the apartment with the groceries.

"Did you see the red van while you waited out front?" asked Sarah.

"I thought I saw a red van drive by as I opened my front door to come over here. It was around the curve by the time I got into the street. I would like to use your phone," Mrs. Greyson added.

"OK," replied Sarah. Sarah showed her to the phone in the bedroom.

Mrs. Greyson called Veny and left him a message to call her.

"I sure thank you for meeting me," said Sarah. "Would you like to join me for supper? We can eat in or eat out."

"I would like that very much," replied Mrs. Greyson. "Let's eat out, and I'll drive. It seems that the driver of the red van knows your car."

"Well, that would be fine."

Chapter 25

Elliot had just returned from his Thursday morning workout when the phone rang. Recognizing the voice as Henry's, he knew what he wanted.

"Yes, I have half the money, if that's what you called about," said Elliot.

"You're a smart boy," replied Henry. "I want to collect it this morning. I'll be taking a stroll along the Charles around nine. I want you to join me. I'll wait for you at the footbridge at the end of Fairfield."

"I'll have it," said Elliot. "See you at nine."

Elliot didn't have to go to the bank to get the money. He kept the cash hidden in a vase on the top shelf in the pantry. Elliot figured that if robbers did break into his condo, they would never think to look in the vase unless if they found it. He showered, put on his jogging clothes and a money belt containing the cash. Locking the door to his condo, Elliot took the elevator to the lobby. He went to the curb and looked both ways before crossing Boylston, then he jogged through the commons and the garden, stopping at the garden's gate on Commonwealth to decide which would be the best way to Fairfield from there. He didn't want to run into Jason on Commonwealth. Elliot continued on Arlington to Beacon Street where he turned left. Elliot slowed to a trot about a block before he reached Fairfield.

At Fairfield, Elliot crossed to the other side and jogged to the footbridge. From where he stood, he didn't see Henry. He strolled across the bridge. Elliot scanned the scene in front of him as he descended the steps, spotting Henry and his two bodyguards on the other side of the pond.

There were not many people here at this time of the day. But in about two hours, the people who worked around here would be eating their lunch, sitting on the nearby benches, and some sunbathing on the grass. The elderly ladies and retired men would be walking their dogs around the pond. Some of the nearby residents would be running and jogging on the path along the Charles River. It would be a very busy place then.

Right now, one jogger passed Henry and his company and himself. Elliot started jogging toward Henry and met him in front of a bench.

"Hey, is that a disguise?" Henry quipped when Elliot stopped a few feet away.

"Where's the dough?"

"Right here," replied Elliot patting the money belt under his jacket.

"Let's see it."

Elliot opened his jacket revealing the money belt. He unzipped it and took out three envelopes. Elliot took his time in handing them to Henry. Henry quickly opened one envelope to check if money was really in it. Then he tore open the other two. Money was in both of them.

"You did well, Elliot. Remember, the rest of it Sunday morning. I'll call you to let you know where I'll be taking my stroll. We'll walk you to the bridge."

As Elliot started up the steps to the bridge, he heard Henry say, "What are you going to do when your cousin takes over the estate and the business? How are you going to raise the cash to pay me back on your loan?"

Elliot didn't like what he was hearing. What did Henry know? He faced Henry and said, "Why should my cousin take over the estate and the business?"

"I've heard a codicil by your uncle has shown up, naming Sarah Edmonds as heir to his estate," replied Henry.

"I think you heard wrong," Elliot shot back.

"Your late uncle's lawyer showed a friend of mine the codicil which your uncle wrote the day before he died, naming your cousin Sarah as sole heir to his fortunes. You're going to have to be real nice to cousin Sarah. Too bad she's married, Elliot," Henry smirked.

Henry turned away with his bodyguards following close behind. As Elliot climbed the steps, he could hear Henry laughing.

When Elliot reached the top of the stairs, he turned to see if Henry and his bodyguards were still around. They weren't—they had vanished.

So the news is out. I wonder if anyone knows she's Uncle Bill's illegitimate daughter, thought Elliot. He'd better sell what he could now of the homeplace if what Henry said was true. *However, I do have certain legal means I can exercise to block Sarah's inheritance. I had better start working on it. The fact she is illegitimate may keep her from inheriting anything.*

Chapter 26

Henry watched the sailboats on the Charles River as his chauffeured silver Jaguar glided along Storrow Drive and then onto Harvard Bridge.

One of the bodyguards sat in front with the driver while Henry and his assistant, Ed, sat in the backseat. Two other bodyguards followed in a dark green Volvo sedan. Of the three cars in Henry's garage, the silver Jaguar was his favorite. He bought it when he made his first million ten years ago. It was a present to himself for enduring fourteen years of grinding, grueling, and sometimes dangerous work. Henry allowed himself very few frills during those days. He and his company had some lean years but now he was rock solid and could afford a few luxuries.

Another of his extravagances was his tenth-floor, four-bedroom, four-bath condo with a large balcony overlooking the Charles River. Henry relished sitting on the balcony, even on cold winter days. He figured he had come a long way during his forty-eight years from near poverty to one of the richest men on the East Coast. His only regret was Heather, his wife, was not here to share all of this with him. He missed her and often wished there was something he could have done to prevent her death.

"Elliot's getting a big head," Henry advised Ed. "He's dreaming too big since he's got a hold of his uncle's billions. We need to keep him in his place. I've heard rumors he's planning to open a casino in town."

"Then you got the phone message I left you," volunteered Ed.

"I thought that sounded like you. Sounded like you were in a hurry too."

"Yeah. I got a little careless and some of Benny's boys caught me going through his office. I gave them the slip long enough to call you from a pay phone to give you the info I discovered from the papers on the desk."

"I wish you wouldn't do that. With the technology we have today, it's not necessary to rummage through desks and files of our competitors." Henry raised his voice. "You're going to get yourself killed one of these days."

"Don't worry. I took advantage of this technology and planted a few bugs while I was going through the office. I've set up a listening station in the backroom of our main office."

"That's good, but don't break into offices anymore. Let one of the younger guys do it. Teach them the finer points of breaking and entering. You're my assistant now and I need to use your skills in other ways."

"Teaching the younger guys, huh?" Ed was downcast.

"Don't feel that way. Both of us are moving up the ladder. We have to delegate many of the jobs we use to do because we are picking up new responsibilities as we move along in our careers. Besides, I don't want to hear that you were killed trashing someone's office. I don't want you to go before me. I can't get along without you. You and me built this business together. Understand? Twenty-five years of hard work."

"Yeah, but it's hard to give up the old ways."

"Yeah. But if we're going to continue our success, we both have to grow with the business. That makes me think of Elliot. We'll take a cruise this weekend and pay him a visit at Monrose. He won't expect us. He's a thorn in our side, and we need to get rid of him. That's your area. Bring anyone you need to help you. Call the marina and tell them we'll be taking the yacht out. Make sure it's in shape for our outing. Tell Maria to call the caterers for the food."

"I haven't told you the latest news from our accountant. It seems Elliot short-changed our gun dealer when he took the shipment to Ireland last month. Skimmed off fifteen grand. Does he think we're stupid? McLeod was furious but I got him pacified."

"Thank you for doing that. I heard about it later," Henry remarked. "That reminds me. Call our associate in Atlanta when we get home. I have a little job for him," said Henry. "I've heard Jason is going to visit Sarah this weekend. We should have a welcoming party for them in Atlanta."

Both Henry and Ed smiled at each other. Ed nodded. This was the kind of work he liked. The Jaguar pulled into the side entrance of an art gallery. The bodyguard jumped out as it slowed down and opened the back door for Henry and Ed.

Ed surveyed the full parking lot. "Looks like your renaissance art exhibit is going over big."

Chapter 27

Elliot was pleased with himself. He was going to have the rest of the payoff for Henry on Sunday. He found two antique dealers who were not afraid of Henry. No one would be at the house tonight. This was Alice's night out and Ernie would be with his bowling league. The first dealer would be there at eight thirty and the other dealer at nine tonight.

The moon shone brightly on the ocean. The few boats in the harbor cast shadows upon the water. There was a brisk breeze and the smell of salt air filled Elliot's nostrils. Not wanting anyone to see him at the house, Elliot parked his BMW in a lane that ran along the estate. He dressed in black pants and a turtleneck so he would blend with the dark. No one used the lane at night, which ended at the cliff overlooking the ocean. Running to the gate in the brick wall, Elliot let himself onto the grounds. He scanned the house.

Good, he thought. The light at the side door was on, which meant Alice was out. He surveyed the house. No other lights were on. *So far, so good.* Elliot dashed to the side entrance. He went to the corner back of the house and climbed over the four-foot wall that ran between the house and the cliff. He had to be careful here since there was only two feet of earth extending from this part of the house. One misstep and he would be on the rocks below. Making it safely to the porch, he jumped onto the pink marble floor from the banister. Elliot stood for a few minutes listening to the waves lap against the rocks below, then he entered the house through the french doors. By the time Elliot reached the front door, he heard a truck coming up the driveway. He opened the door and stood in the dark hall.

It was just a few minutes after the first truck left, when the second dealer arrived in a small moving van. Elliot escorted him and his assistant into the living room. Only a few items remained of Uncle Bill's collection when they left.

A light was on in the living room of the big house when Ernie pulled into the carriage house parking area. He knew it was too early for Alice to be back from the movies, so he went over to check out the place. A moving van was at the front door. *Strange. I wonder* . . . . Ernie eased up to a living room window on the garden side of the mansion. He kept quiet.

Ernie pressed his body along the wall next to the window and leaned his head to the side to peer through the window. Elliot received money from a tall man in overalls who appeared to be in his forties. The other fellow was a young man about twenty years old, Ernie guessed. They shook hands and left the room. A few minutes later, Ernie heard the moving van start up and then move down the driveway. The light went out in the living room.

Elliot hurried to the study. He turned on the desk lamp and opened the safe. He pulled an envelope from a desk drawer, stuffed the money into it, and placed it in the safe. Elliot closed and locked the door to the safe and turned off the desk lamp. He left the house through the side door, being careful to lock it.

Ernie moved quietly along the front of the house. He arrived at the front corner to see Elliot run across the side yard to the gate, open it, and disappear. Ernie heard a car start up as he ran toward the gate. He got to the lane in time to see a dark car speed away. Elliot didn't have the car's lights on.

He had an idea what Elliot was doing here, but he wanted to make sure. Ernie let himself in the front door with Alice's extra key. He flipped on the hall light, hurrying to the living room. Ernie turned on the lamp on the table nearest the door. The shelves that held Mr. Monrose's collection were empty except for two small china ducks. Ernie was disgusted and called Mr. Abbott.

Chapter 28

"Pam, the new leasing agent at the office, called me late yesterday to say the red Ford van doesn't belong to anyone living here and neither does the green Corolla," Mrs. Greyson told Sarah.

She, Sarah, and Charlie strolled to the mailboxes in the gazebo in the center of their apartment complex.

"Veny traced the van through its license number," continued Mrs. Greyson. "They've found it and are keeping a watch on it."

"Aren't they going to arrest the driver?" Sarah asked.

"No. Veny and his supervisor want to watch the van for a while. I don't need to tell you not to repeat any of what I'm telling."

"No. I won't tell anyone. I guess they want to find out who the guy is working with."

"You're right," stated Mrs. Greyson.

"With all the excitement, I forgot to tell you Jason will be here tomorrow. I'm going to meet him at the airport. His plane arrives between eleven and eleven-thirty. I want you to meet him. Maybe we can get together for supper Saturday night?"

"That'll be fine with me. I would love to meet this handsome guy of yours."

"That reminds me. I need to look at a map to see how to get to the airport. It's been a year since I have been there."

"It has been many years since I have been out there. I usually take a bus when I travel out of state. I don't care that much for flying. Why don't you call the airport for directions? I'm sure they'll be glad to help you."

"That's a thought," replied Sarah.

Sarah and Mrs. Greyson collected the mail from their respective boxes and went back to their apartments together. Mrs. Greyson invited Sarah into her place for tea and cookies. She and Sarah spent about an hour looking through Mrs. Greyson's scrapbooks on Roswell.

Jason bounded down the steps of his workplace a few minutes before quitting time. He wanted to get home to pack a few things for his weekend trip to Atlanta. Jason was happy with anticipation of seeing Sarah tomorrow. He decided to take the subway from the Arlington Street station instead of walking through the garden and the commons to the Park Street station.

Jason had just turned the corner from Commonwealth onto Arlington. He was in front of the Ritz-Carton when he turned around. He felt that he was being watched. He spotted Elliot standing on the corner where he was only a few seconds before. Elliot was watching him but didn't make a move to greet him. Jason turned around and kept on going. As he descended down the station steps, he felt as if a hole was being bored into his back. He turned around and Elliot was still there watching him with scorn.

Jason turned and continued into the station, escaping the hate flowing from Elliot.

Chapter 29

"**M**r. Abbot! I gather you've been here for most of the night," Chris exclaimed as she entered the reception area of the office. Larry stood at the coffeepot across from her desk. His jacket lay across the sofa and his tie draped across the lamp on her desk. Larry's shirt collar was open and he sported an after-five shadow.

"Yes. It seems that the courier didn't deliver those papers to Elliot Winter last night. I called the courier service, and they explained they went to his office and his condo several times. He wasn't in. The reason they couldn't find him was because he was at the mansion selling off Bill's antique collection," Larry stormed. "Ernie called me last night after he saw Elliot leave the mansion." Larry paused as he sipped his coffee.

"I'm waiting for a call from the courier that he has delivered them to Elliot. He is waiting outside of his condo building."

"That's a shame. Do you think any of the items can be recovered?"

"I don't know. Don is checking on that now."

"Have you had anything to eat this morning?" Chris inquired.

"Well, no."

"I'll go across the street and get some donuts and bagels."

"Thank you. I'm getting a little hungry. I'll take a couple of apple and cheese danish. And bring a few extra donuts and bagels for our clients. Mr. Wells will be here in an hour and his representatives from the car company will be arriving around 10:30."

As Chris was going out the door, Larry called to her, "And when you return, please get Jason Edmonds for me. He should be at home getting ready to leave for Atlanta. I want to share the latest Elliot escapade with him."

"OK, I will," said Chris as she disappeared around the door and down the hall.

The phone rang as Larry entered his office.

"Hello."

"That's good. You finally served those papers. Where did you catch up with him?"

"At his office." Pause. "He just laughed and said I was too late," Larry repeated. "Hum."

"Well, thank you." He sighed with exasperation. *What an ugly mess.*

Chapter 30

Sarah had a good night's sleep. When the radio alarm came on this morning, Ginger was curled up next to her. Not wanting to disturb the cat, Sarah slipped out quietly on the other side of the bed. She turned off the radio and went into the kitchen to prepare the roast beef for the Crock-Pot. Jason enjoyed roast beef, and Sarah was preparing all of Jason's favorites for supper tonight. It's going to be a really good Friday night supper. Sarah made two pumpkin pies before turning in last night. She found herself singing throughout the morning preparations. Ginger followed her everywhere, purring her own song.

Nine o'clock already, thought Sarah, as she checked the clock in the kitchen.

"I had better start getting ready to leave for the airport. Jason's plane gets in at 11:15, so I want to be there by 10:30," Sarah explained to Ginger. "It'll give me a few extra minutes in case I make the wrong turn somewhere along the way."

Exhilarated with Jason's arrival, Sarah forgot about the red van. She thought only of Jason and the good time they would have together this weekend. Sarah wondered if Jason had heard anything more about Uncle Bill's will. With these thoughts floating in her head, she was oblivious to the red van parked by the office as she drove by, or notice that it followed three cars behind her as she went down Holcomb Bridge Road and then headed down GA 400. Another car fell in behind the red van on I-75. By the time Sarah passed Martin Luther King, Jr. Boulevard, there were four cars following her.

Sarah was delighted she made the right turn from I-85 to the airport. The airport had not changed. She now knew where she was and looked for the garage parking. As Sarah pulled up to the gate to take a ticket, she saw the red van pull up behind her in the rearview mirror. Then a white sedan and a blue pickup truck pulled up on each side of her. Sarah saw the door of the white sedan on her left swing open. She grabbed the ticket from the machine as the gate opened and she gunned her Corolla up the ramp with her heart pounding.

The van driver got back in, crashed the closing gate to follow her up the ramp. The blue pickup truck on the left moved to block the garage entrance while the white sedan followed the red van.

As Sarah passed the entrance to the second floor parking, a car pulled out with red lights flashing. She heard the screeching of tires and then metal hitting metal. Looking through the rearview mirror, Sarah saw policemen pull two people out of the van. Then she heard sirens. As Sarah pulled onto the roof, she was greeted by an airport security car and a police car.

Veny stepped out of the police car. Then Sarah grasped what was going on. She was glad to see Veny. Her heart began to slow down to a normal beat. Sarah let out a huge sigh as Veny approached her. Her body relaxed.

"Well, Sarah," said Veny, "it looks like we got 'em. We've been watching you since last night. Grandmom told me you would be going to the airport today, so we thought we would follow along when we saw the red van park at the office this morning."

"At the office? Thoroughbred Acres?" she inquired. "Oh my. I had forgotten all about the red van. I was so caught up with Jason's visit this weekend. How can I thank you? I sure do appreciate your taking care of me."

"It's our job to take care of the citizens. We're glad to do it anytime." Veny winked an eye and added, "A pumpkin pie would be welcome at our house."

"A pumpkin pie?" Sarah replied surprised.

"Yep."

Sarah laughed, realizing Veny was kidding.

"Your grandmom is a good detective. She saw those cans of pumpkin when we put the groceries up last night."

He laughed. "Go on and meet your husband. We'll talk to you later," said Veny.

"Thanks again," Sarah called out to Veny as he got back into the police car.

Sarah parked the car and observed the time on the dashboard clock. *Jason's plane is landing in about ten minutes!* She hurried across the parking lot into the terminal. Locating the information desk, she inquired the gate number were Jason's plane would be debarking. Hearing it, Sarah took off running, leaving the information agent talking.

Sarah laid her handbag on the belt to go through security. The tension was building. She didn't want to miss Jason. She hurried through the gate. The alarm made several loud beeps as the handbag passed through the X-ray machine. The security guard on the other side of the gate grabbed her handbag and blocked her passage. "Is this your handbag, ma'am?"

"Yes," replied Sarah. *Oh no,* she thought. *Jason's plane is landing now.*

"Please step over here. I'm going to have to search it since the alarm went off."

"I'll be glad to take everything out of it," said Sarah, as she took out her wallet and comb and laid it on the table next to the handbag.

"Please don't, ma'am. I'm conducting the search and I know what I'm looking for."

Sarah ceased helping and waited for him to complete the search of her handbag.

"Everything seems to be OK, ma'am. You can go now," said the security guard.

"Thank you," said Sarah. She hurriedly picked up her wallet, comb, compact, keys, and other possessions and threw them into her purse as she moved quickly to the escalators.

I hope I don't miss him, Sarah thought.

The train pulled up just as Sarah reached the entrance to the train stop. Sarah enjoyed the ride. It brought back memories of her and Jason's first plane trip to Atlanta. They were impressed with the train's computerized voice. They both agreed a computerized voice announcing the stops was what the Boston Green Line needed.

Sarah got off at C Terminal and followed the crowd up the escalators. Looking around, she saw the sign that directed her to Gate 15.

As she hurried to the gate, Sarah looked at the travelers going in the opposite direction to see if Jason was among them. People were standing around Gate 15 as she approached. Sarah observed that the entry door to the plane ramp was closed. Locating the monitor over the ticket desk, Sarah learned the plane was late. The landing time was 12: 05. *Well,* she thought, *I have a few minutes to spare. What a morning!* She hoped the rest of this day would be uneventful. She wanted for them to have a relaxing, enjoyable weekend together. She felt their lives were changing yet again. Their lives definitely wouldn't be the same after Monday.

Soon, the door opened and passengers were crowding into the waiting area, pushing by the ticket counter, and many being met by friends and relatives standing around her. Sarah knew Jason would be the last one, or close to the last one, off the plane. The flight must have been full, Sarah thought, as the passengers kept coming through the door. Then there he was. His six-foot-four frame made him easy to spot, a handsome guy with short-trimmed black hair and clear blue eyes. Sarah wanted to hug him at that moment. But there were about fifty people between her and Jason, so she waved to him. He saw her and threw her a kiss. She pretended to catch it and put it in her pocket.

Jason was so happy to see Sarah he hugged and kissed her before he even said hello. They walked hand in hand down the corridor, oblivious to all around them. Talking, laughing, and then being quiet for a few moments. They stopped at the baggage carrousel and picked up his garment bag. They stood there for a few moments talking. Then Sarah suggested they had better get going.

Sarah told him on the train about the drug dealers following her to the airport and their arrest by the police. She said she would tell him the rest later. That was fine with Jason. He was grateful she was all right. He knew Sarah was still excited although she tried to hide it. He hugged her again.

"Can I carry something?" Sarah inquired.

"I think I can manage," Jason replied.

"That garment bag is bulky. I'll take your briefcase."

Sarah grabbed it from Jason's hand before he could protest.

"Ha, ha, I got it. Isn't it better sharing the load?" Sarah asked. "What have you got in it anyway? It's heavy," pretending to fall partway to the floor with it.

"You know, the usual—books, shoes, etc."

"It feels like you've got the kitchen sink in here."

Jason grinned.

They went out of the terminal, crossed the street to the rooftop of the garage where Sarah had parked the Corolla.

"Where did you park the car?" Jason asked Sarah.

"It's on the other side of the roof. At the time I parked it, I was excited from the commotion at the ticket gate. I hope I parked it in a parking space. I hope I didn't leave it sitting in the middle of a lane. There's a wall that divides the roof. There are several places for pedestrians to walk through."

"I'm sure you did OK. I wonder how I would have done under those circumstances?" Jason commented.

At that moment, a black limousine pulled alongside of Jason and a dark blue Continental pulled alongside of Sarah. The doors of both cars opened, and the guys stepping out held guns. The one in the limousine motioned for them to get in.

"Not again," Sarah said. "I'm not getting in. Once is enough today."

"Get in," said the guy with the gun.

Jason knew Sarah wouldn't get in. He waited to see what she was going to do. Then his briefcase came up.

Sarah swung the briefcase to her right, knocking the guy with the gun back against the Continental. Then quickly she swung it to her left, barely missing Jason as he ducked, hitting the guy standing next to him. The guy dropped his gun; and as he did, Jason grabbed it, glad for his military experience in the Gulf War.

"Run, Sarah, run," Jason commanded. Sarah hesitated. "Run," Jason shouted. Sarah ran for the wall that divided the garage roof. She heard a car coming quickly up behind her, then a loud pop and a screeching of wheels. *Just a few more feet to the wall,* Sarah thought. *Run, run, run,* she told herself.

As Sarah approached the wall, she saw an airport security car. She waved to it. *They can't see me,* thought Sarah. She waved again as she came through the pedestrian walk between the wall. The security car speeded toward her.

She told them briefly what happened when they stopped next to her. They saw the Continental and watched as armed men climbed out of it. Within seconds, the airport security police were out of the car running toward them with guns drawn. Sarah was close on their heels. The Continental backed up and fled down the nearest ramp.

Jason was crouched behind a car parked parallel with the limousine. The gunmen opened fire on the security police who took cover behind parked cars. Sarah ducked behind a Ford pickup. She peeked around the truck looking for Jason. The gunmen were scrambling into the limousine when the security police returned fire. One guy fell to the ground. The limousine careened with terrific speed, leaving another guy behind. He ran for the exit to the next level while the security police checked the one lying on the ground. He heard his fallen buddy tell the security police that Elliot Winter was his employer. He then continued his flight down the stairs with a big grin.

About two hours later, Sarah and Jason were walking across the roof of the garage to their car.

"I can't believe those guys tried to abduct us," Sarah said.

"Neither can I," commented Jason.

"It's hard for me to believe Elliot was behind it. But Lieutenant Sanburn said the wounded man told them Elliot was his boss. It doesn't make sense."

"No, it doesn't. However, he's been involved with some shady characters. From what I gathered from Uncle Bill, he gambled a lot and made bad investments. I forgot to tell you Larry called me before I left this morning to tell me Elliot had sold Bill's travel collection."

"Oh no," moaned Sarah. "I wonder if he has sold anything else."

"Larry has a private investigator keeping watch on the mansion." He didn't tell her Larry was also discreetly inquiring of the corporation's accounting department if any funds were missing.

They both walked quietly for a few minutes, then Jason said, "I thought the police would never quit asking us questions."

"Me too," replied Sarah.

They reached the car and loaded Jason's luggage into the trunk. Sarah was grateful to Jason when he volunteered to drive home.

As they climbed into the car, Sarah asked, "Do you want to stop somewhere to eat, or eat the roast I have cooking at home?"

"No more stops. Let's get on home and eat the roast. I'm hungry. By the way, which way do we go home?" Jason asked. Then he began laughing.

Sarah joined him. It was laughter of relief, joy, anxiety. She laughed till tears were in her eyes. Jason wiped the tears with his handkerchief. They hugged and kissed.

"You know, it's quite possible that if those guys succeeded with their plan, we wouldn't be here right now. We may be dead," Jason reflected.

"I know," whispered Sarah. Clearing her throat to regain her voice, "I'm glad we were able to escape. I have some good times planned for us this weekend. Let's not let this episode ruin them."

"I don't plan to, honey," Jason replied. "Let's go home and enjoy that roast you have cooking. I'm hungry. Tomorrow morning I'll be meeting with the firm's clients in Atlanta. They were agreeable to meet on Saturday. We should be finished by noon. Then we'll have the rest of the weekend to ourselves."

"That sounds fine to me."

As they drove out of the airport, Sarah gave him directions to Thoroughbred Acres.

Chapter 31

Elliot drove to the mansion, thinking it strange that a friend of Elaine had left a message on his answering machine. She said Elaine wanted to talk to him and would meet him at the mansion around six. Elliot called Elaine but received only her voice mail. He did want to talk to her so he canceled his dinner plans with the Thompsons. He wondered why she didn't call herself. Well, he would ask when he saw her.

Before leaving the office, he called Alice to ask her to prepare supper for him and Elaine and discovered she was on her way to spend the weekend with an ailing cousin in Springfield. Alice said she received a call about an hour ago and was getting ready to call him to let him know she was going away. She added Ernie also was out for the evening.

Elliot exited Hwy 128 onto Highway 62, driving through Beverly to Latrop Street which runs parallel to the ocean. Turning left, Elliot drove to the stop signal and turned right.

He found the steaks in the refrigerator where Alice said she would leave them to defrost. She had left a box of wild rice and several cans of green beans on the counter for him. Elliot also found the fixings for a lettuce salad in the refrigerator.

We're going to have a good supper tonight, he thought. He put the salad together and placed it in the refrigerator. Then he thought about dessert. *It's about time for Elaine. I'll ask her if she wants dessert.* He went to the front hall door and looked out the panes around it. Not seeing her red convertible, he opened the door and stepped onto the porch. He enjoyed this place. It was serene.

After tomorrow, I'll have Henry paid off and then I can think about moving out here. Sarah's not going to set one foot in here. It's mine by all rights.

Elliot's thoughts were interrupted by a noise. It sounded as if it came from the side of the house. Thinking it might be Elaine parking her car in the carriage house area, Elliot stepped toward the garden path to meet her halfway. From the corner of his eye, he glimpsed a figure close to the cliff were wooden stairs led to the rocky beach below. He turned to face it.

"Hello, there," he called. "Can I help you with anything?"

The figure looked like it was motioning for him to come over. *Strange, he's wearing a dark cap pulled over his head.*

Elliot hesitated. He looked down the path cutting through the garden and didn't see Elaine. He looked to the cliff where the figure stood, but it wasn't there anymore. Curious, he hurried to the cliff to see if he had gone down the steps. Water was filling the rocky beach. It was high tide. No one was in sight. He turned to approach the mansion.

Elaine approached the mansion by the carriage house driveway. She saw Elliot on the front porch as she neared and watched him go around the side of the house. She followed him from the front porch. Elaine came around the corner from the front of the house and saw Elliot standing at the edge of the cliff. She raised her hand to wave to him when a noise at one of the windows caught her attention. Elaine spotted a gloved hand holding a gun. Before she could move, she heard a soft swish and watched Elliot fall backward over the cliff. A black-clad figure jumped out of the window, running past her, pushing the gun into her hand. She got a whiff of a scent. Cologne? The man ran to the beach stairs and disappeared down the steps. She was stunned by what she had just witnessed. She couldn't move.

Voices were coming from the front lawn of the mansion. Then sirens. She shook herself as if to awake from a dream. Elaine fled through the garden carrying the gun. Her car was in front of the carriage house.

Elaine climbed into her car and left by the carriage house entrance. Before pulling onto the road, she looked to the main entrance of the mansion. A few more police cars turned in there. Making sure no cars were coming from either way, Elaine turned onto the road in the opposite direction of the main gate.

Chapter 32

Henry was enjoying the sunset over the ocean on the deck of his yacht when Ed brought him the phone.

"Hello, sir. Sorry I wasn't in when you called."

"That's all right," said Henry. "How did the party go?"

"It got crashed," said the voice, "and one of the guys took a slug."

"So, you didn't get the presents?"

"Right. But Hank heard Sal tell the cops that he worked for Elliot Winter."

"That's great," Henry said happily. "Is he in jail? Has the bond been set?"

"The bond has been set. We'll pay it, and he'll be released in a couple of days. He's in the prison hospital right now."

"You know, it might be a blessing the party was crashed. The cops will add that to Elliot's list of felonies, and we'll be off the hook. That was a great idea of telling the boys to put the blame on Elliot," Henry said.

"By the way, give the guy a bonus for taking the slug," Henry added.

"How did the party go at your end?" asked the voice.

"It went off very well. It seems that there was a prowler at the Monrose mansion when Elliot was there. Someone in a boat happened to be going by the place when he saw someone fall over the cliff. He called the police who happened to be on their way. My source told me someone had also called about a prowler a few minutes before the guy on the boat called the police. Interesting, huh? The source also told me Elliot was shot, but his body hasn't been found," Henry reported.

"It seems that everything has been tied up. And even if Elliot somehow survives, he's wanted for the attempted kidnapping of his cousin. That's brilliant," said the voice. "You thought of everything."

"You and your associates take a vacation for a couple of days until this thing blows over. Put it on my tab. Go down to the islands."

"Well, thank you. We will," said the voice.

Henry hung up the phone and smiled.

"Well, everything today has been a great success. Elliot Winter's budding career has come to an end. That was good thinking when you put the gun in that girl's hand. And thanks to you and your magic fingers, I even have Elliot's final payment for me. We don't need to worry about competition from him anymore," said Henry.

Henry sat in a chair on the deck with Ed standing beside him. They both watched the last red rays of the sun shimmer over the gentle ocean waves in silence.

Yes, it was a profitable day, thought Ed.

Chapter 33

Elaine couldn't keep her hands from shaking as she held on to the steering wheel. Her whole body shook as she drove toward her apartment. *I've got to pull myself together. I've got to think what my next steps should be. I can't stay around here,* she thought. *No. Someone may have seen me. I need to leave here, but I can't go zooming down the road. I've got to slow down. Should I call the police? Would they believe that I didn't shoot Elliot? Maybe not. I have the gun that shot him. The man who gave it to me wore gloves, so only my fingerprints are on it.*

It seemed to take forever to get home—a two-family dwelling where she lived on the top floor and the landlady lived below.

She rented the place furnished, so there wasn't much for her to pack. Elaine liked Mrs. Irvington, the landlady, and hated to leave in such haste. She dashed off a note to Mrs. Irvington, explaining there was a family crisis and had to leave immediately. She knew she probably wouldn't be returning, so she packed up everything and stuffed as much as she could in her convertible. She would get in touch with Mrs. Irvington later about the rest of her belongings.

Elaine wondered what Elliot wanted to talk about. She had a phone message to meet him at Monrose. The voice didn't sound like Elliot though. She decided while driving there that this would be a good time to say good-bye to him. Now he was gone. In a blink of an eye, Elliot had gone over the cliff. *I wonder if he survived,* she reflected.

Heading north, Elaine drove through New Hampshire, listening to the radio for news of Elliot's shooting. *There it was.* She turned the radio up. She listened for any mention of a woman seen leaving the place. *Yes. Yes, someone saw me.* She listened as the radio newsman reported, "A woman was seen leaving the estate shortly before the police arrived. An anonymous phone call to the local police about a shooting at the Monrose mansion sent several police cars to the home. A description of the woman was not given by the police. Reports indicate she's driving a small red convertible. The police are searching the Boston metro area." He went on to the next news story as Elaine pondered what to do now. It was dark, and no one would notice the car on these back roads, she reasoned. Her panic ebbed; she could think a little more clearly. *But I have the gun*—it is in the box of books on the backseat. *What am I going to do with it,* she wondered.

Chapter 34

Ten more minutes before we land at Logan Airport. A lot has happened since I left a month and a half ago. Jason had drifted off to sleep. Or maybe he was pretending. Ginger was sitting on her lap. The hostesses wanted to see the cat. They told her it was all right to take the cat out of the carrier once they were in the air. Ginger enjoyed all the attention and was good about staying in her lap and Jason's.

Larry called them Saturday morning to tell them of Elliot's death.

"The authorities think he's dead but they haven't found the body," Sarah remembered Larry saying.

Even though she and Elliot didn't agree on many things, she was saddened by his death. She remembered the times they played in the tree behind his house and taking riding lessons with him. Those were fun times, but things changed when they were teens. Elliot became possessive of her when she was fifteen. He wouldn't let her go out with anyone but him. He made sure the guys knew Sarah was his girlfriend.

Elliot's possessiveness came to a head with Rob who shared several classes with Sarah. Sarah found Rob very attractive and smart. They had been on several dates. One Saturday night, they went to the movies. On the way home, they had stopped at a local ice cream shop and were enjoying frappes when Elliot showed up. He charged through the shop's door. The place was crowded. Sarah saw Elliot before Rob did from their table close to the back. He shot Sarah an angry look. Elliot was on Rob before she had a chance to warn him. He pulled Rob up from the chair and shouted at him, "That's my girlfriend. No one goes out with her but me."

"She can go out with anyone she wants," Rob shot back.

"That's right, Elliot," Sarah agreed. Elliot hit Rob with his right fist connecting with his face. Rob staggered a little from the blow, then swung and gave Elliot a good blow to the stomach. Sarah shouted at them to quit. Several guys pulled them apart. Rob grabbed Sarah's hand and they left. Outside, they could hear Elliot cursing Rob. A couple of weeks later, Rob was in an accident that kept him out of school for several months. Sarah always suspected Elliot to be responsible for that.

Sarah and Rob explained to her parents that night what Elliot did. She was thankful that they had understood. Elliot was mad and stalked her for the rest of the school year. Sarah's parents talked to Anne, Elliot's mother, and Bill about the situation. Anne and Bill sent Elliot to a private boarding school in western Massachusetts that fall where he stayed until he graduated. They could've gone to the police, but this was a family affair, and the Monroses' took care of their own problems. Since her marriage to Jason, Elliot rarely spoke to her. *Now he's presumed dead,* thought Sarah. *I like to think of him as the way he was when we were kids, not what he has turned into. As Jason often tells me, "I wear blinders where he's concerned." I guess he's right.*

Later that Saturday, Veny dropped by and got Sarah's statement about the airport incident. Veny said he heard about the kidnapping attempt. He explained that one of the guys he and his group had arrested at the airport was a Roswell policeman. During the few days he and his supervisor had watched him, he led them to the others in the ring. Two of those were policemen too. Veny was upset to find his coworkers involved in drugs. He explained that the Roswell policeman drove the red Ford van. The policeman admitted he thought Sarah could identify him, so he was trying to get rid of her.

How close I came to not being here with Ginger and Jason. Well, I'm here and very grateful. And look down there. There's George's Island. And there's the lighthouse. "We're home, Ginger." Jason woke up, and they both listened to the hostess instruct everyone to fasten their seat belts and make sure all the tables were in their proper position.

"Let's put Ginger in her carrier," Jason said. Sarah pulled the carrier out from under the seat in front of her. She held it while Jason put Ginger inside. Ginger didn't struggle this time. *I guess she knows she's home,* thought Sarah.

A few bumps announced that the plane was on the ground, and then it was taxiing to the gate. People started unbuckling their seat belts and standing up in the aisle to get their belongings out of the overhead bins.

Sarah, Jason, and Ginger were the last to leave the plane. Jason had left his Volvo at the airport garage. They got their luggage. Jason got the car while Sarah and Ginger waited outside the terminal. Within twenty minutes, they were on their way home to Salem. They had about two hours before their meeting with Larry.

Chapter 35

Larry was talking to Chris when Sarah and Jason entered the outer office.
"Hello, Mr. and Mrs. Edmonds," Chris said smiling.

"So good to see you both," said Larry. "I hope you had a good flight."

"We did," replied Jason. "No surprises waiting for us at Logan. Very grateful for that."

"I hadn't planned on welcoming Jason that way in Atlanta," Sarah laughed. "I think we both have had enough adventure to do us for a while."

"Let's go in," Larry said, as he motioned them to go into his office.

Sarah and Jason sat in armchairs positioned in front of Larry's desk. Larry sat behind the desk and opened a folder lying in front of him.

"Well, we know why we're here," Larry proceeded.

"Is anyone else included in the change?" Sarah asked.

"Ernie and Alice and everything else is the same as in the previous will. The only change is with regard to you, Sarah, and Elliot. According to your uncle's codicil, everything that went to Elliot now goes to you."

Larry read the codicil to Sarah and Jason.

It took a few minutes for the words to sink in. Then Sarah thought aloud, "Elliot has nothing now. I don't know how to feel about this. Larry, do you know what prompted Uncle Bill to make this change?"

"I think Elliot did something that made him mad. Very mad. Bill called me the day before he died and said he had written a codicil to his will, cutting Elliot out of everything. He said Elliot was not the right person to run Monrose Industries. He asked me to come over Sunday afternoon to discuss Elliot and the change. As you know, Bill didn't live long enough to tell me."

Jason said with a smile, "Well, honey, you don't have to look for a job any longer."

"You're right! You're right, I don't! Running Monrose Industries is going to be more than enough to keep me busy. I hope I'm up to it. I have a lot of reading ahead of me to catch up with what is going on in the business world and with Monrose Industries. Maybe I should hire someone to run it. No, no. I want to try my hand at this.

"Well, I'm with you all the way," said Jason.

"I remember Bill asking me if I wanted to take over when he retired or passed on. I thought the suggestion was funny. I couldn't see myself at the head of the business. Besides," Sarah looked at Jason, "we had been married only a month and Uncle Bill had wanted me to start learning the business then. I told him I had other interests. I really preferred working with book publishers." A pause. "I think I am ready now to take on the responsibilities of the corporation." She sighed. "Our life is going to be changed," Sarah mused.

"Probably more than you realize," Larry added.

"Jason, would you want to help me run the corporation? Leave your career in architecture? I know how much you love your work. But I was wondering . . ." Sarah picked up Jason's hand and held it in hers.

"Let me think about it, sweetie. This is so sudden." Jason squeezed her hand.

"I understand. We both have a lot to think about and decisions to make." Sarah smiled at Jason.

"Mr. Abbot, how is the transition going to take place?" Sarah let Jason's hand go, putting her hand back into her lap.

"I have taken the liberty of notifying the board that there's a new owner. The chairman said he and the other members would like to meet with you as soon as possible. So I have arranged for you to meet with the board members next Thursday. You know the chairman, William Grant Adams. He wants to take you on a tour of the facilities when you're ready."

"Oh yes. I met him last year at the Publisher's Expo in Reading. He seems to be very capable of handling his responsibilities." A pause. Sarah sighs. "It's hard to believe Elliot's dead." Jason gathered Sarah's hand into his. He didn't share Sarah's feelings for Elliot, yet he respected them. Jason hoped that maybe someday she'll see Elliot for what he was.

"Is there anything else you have questions about?" Larry inquired.

"I can't think of anything right now. Can you, Jason?"

"No, honey, I can't."

"On to the next item," said Larry.

"Now, Sarah, Bill has left a letter for you and has requested you read it at the time the codicil is read. It came in the envelope with it. I have read the letter. Before we continue any further, Jason and I will retire to the outer office so you can read it in private."

Larry motioned Jason to leave. Jason stood up and then put his hand on Sarah's shoulder for a moment and then left with Larry.

Sarah looked at the envelope and took out the letter. She recognized her uncle's handwriting. *I wonder what this is all about. So mysterious.* She began to read.

Dear Sarah,

I don't know of any good way to tell you what I am going to tell you. Your adoptive parents, my brother and his wife, had planned to tell you many times. But they didn't want to upset you. You were so happy. Yes, Sarah, you are adopted. What my brother and his wife didn't know was that I am your father.

I hope you can forgive me for not coming forward before now. I was grateful to have you close to me. I could watch you and enjoy you as you grew into a young woman. How happy I was when you took the honors in your high school graduation. Happier still when you finished college. And I was very happy for you on your wedding day. You were a beautiful bride. You and Jason are a handsome couple. You chose well when you chose Jason to share your life with. He is a good man, as you already know.

I have wonderful memories of you learning to wear high heels and taking riding lessons at Ridder's Stables. I wanted so much to tell you that I am your father. But I thought it best that your adoptive parents tell you before I said anything to you or to them about who your real parents are. It's been difficult, Sarah.

You probably want to know about your mother. She loved you very much, but she had to give you up. Your mother's name is Margaret. We grew up together; and in our junior year at high school, we promised to marry each other when we graduated from college. We never married, though. The last year at college, Margaret met a fellow during the holidays when she visited her aunt. After we graduated, I became involved in the family business. Even though we were officially engaged by then, there were times I didn't see Margaret for two or three weeks at a time because of the business. She understood. We had planned to be married in the summer a year after graduation. We started looking for a house and Margaret was looking at dresses and putting together a list of things we needed to do for the wedding.

I became very involved with the company that winter, doing some traveling. January that year, Margaret came to me and told me she was pregnant. I told her that we could move the wedding up. Then she told me that she loved someone else. He knew she was pregnant by me but he wanted to marry her anyway. But she had to give up the child. He didn't want another man's child.

Margaret was in agony. She loved him. And she wanted the child. I was stunned. I told her we should think about this for a few days. Then we'd get together and talk about it some more. She agreed.

I was grieved, my dear. A thought came to me during those few days. My brother and his wife had wanted children. But they didn't have any after three years of marriage. The thought came to me to approach them about adopting a baby. And I went so far as to tell them of a woman I knew who was expecting a child but, due to circumstances, couldn't keep it. They liked the thought and we went forward with the plan. I told Margaret at our next meeting what had transpired. She was relieved my brother and his wife wanted our baby. She was happy. She left a month later to live with her aunt until her wedding a few weeks later. I promised her I would never tell anyone about you, except you, if you ever needed to know.

I love you, my dear Sarah. Throughout our lives, I had to be an uncle to you, not a father. I am grateful, though, I did have you close to me. Please forgive, Sarah, for any wrong that I may have done to you. All I want for you is your happiness.

If you remember, we had talked about the possibility of you taking over the corporation when I was ready to step down or if I died before then, shortly after you married Jason. I thought then you would be good for the company. I respected your wishes and named Elliot as my heir.

I have changed my will, as you will know when you read this, for I have asked Larry to give you this letter upon my death. You are the legal heir to the family fortune and business. I wish you well, my dearest daughter.

With all my love, your father,
William A. Monrose

The envelope also contained a copy of her birth certificate.

Sarah was astounded. Attempted kidnapping, now a fortune—and, and another set of parents; biological parents. *Oh my. It's too much for me*, Sarah thought. *No, no. I just need some time to think. To get used to Uncle Bill as a father. To get used to the inheritance. I wished my parents had told me that I was adopted. That would not have bothered me. I could have taken it better then than now. Then maybe I could've spent more time with Uncle Bill.* Tears trickled down Sarah's cheeks. *I wonder about my mother. Is she still alive? Where does she live? Oh, goodness. Maybe there is a reason this turned out this way. Maybe God is working his purpose out. I have dozens of questions for Mr. Abbot. My life has certainly changed. I'm glad that I have Jason for my best friend. Together, we'll make it.*

The door opened, and Jason entered. "How are you, honey?"

"I don't know. This letter is from my father. Uncle Bill was my father. Here, you can read it," Sarah said as she handed the letter to Jason. She pulled a tissue from her purse and wiped the tears from her face and eyes.

She watched him read it. She could tell it surprised him as it had her.

"What can I say?" Jason said after reading the letter.

"I don't know." Sarah shrugged.

Sarah got up from her chair and came over to Jason. He gave her the letter which she put back into the envelope and then placed it into her purse. "This certainly is a family of secrets," commented Sarah.

"It's been a long day, my sweet man. It's getting late, and I am getting hungry. I have lots of questions. Let's think about these things later." Jason put an arm around Sarah's waist to escort her out of the office.

"Let's stop at Weylus in Saugus on the way home," suggested Jason.

"You're reading my mind," replied Sarah, smiling.

Sarah spent a few minutes talking to Mr. Abbot. He volunteered to help her find answers to her questions. She wasn't angry with her parents or Uncle Bill—maybe she should be. Right now, she was shocked; and when the shock wears off, she'll decide whether she wanted to dig any deeper.

Chapter 36

Anne didn't know what to think. The news reports gave the impression Elliot was dead. But the reporters kept saying that his body had not been found. Because his body hadn't been found, Anne believed he was still alive. Somewhere . . . he is somewhere. Someone had found him. *I believe someone must have found him. But why haven't they taken him to a hospital or called the police?*

Her thoughts were interrupted when the phone rang.

"Hello," Anne answered. "Oh, Gladys! I'm glad to hear your voice. You've heard then about Elliot? . . . I would be so glad if you came over," Anne replied. "No. No one from the media has called . . . You think so? Oh, I hope not. I don't want to be bothered by them . . . OK. I'll see you in about fifteen minutes."

She hung up the phone, went into the sunroom, and sat down on the sofa.

"My dear, dear Elliot, what have you gotten yourself into?" Anne lamented aloud. "I know you're not an angel, but I didn't think you would get yourself so deep into trouble that your life would come to this. I pray you are alive, Elliot. And I pray that if you ever get out of this ordeal, you will turn your life around. Leave whatever evil you're involved in."

Anne shed a few tears and then, looking at the violets, realized she hadn't watered them today. She went to the kitchen and got the watering can from beneath the sink and filled it with water. She was watering the violets and thinking about Elliot when Gladys rang the doorbell.

Gladys gave Anne a hug when she got inside the door.

"I'm so sorry that you're having to go through all of this," Gladys said. Gladys and Anne had known each other all their lives. They went to the same school up to the sixth grade, when Gladys's parents moved to the next town. But that didn't keep them apart. They had shopped for their prom dresses together and later their bridal dresses. Gladys was there when Anne's husband passed away. And Anne was there with Gladys when her husband Ben passed on just three years ago.

"Well, Gladys, it's a lot easier with you by my side," replied Anne.

"I hate to tell you this, but I saw a TV news van four blocks from here. I hope they aren't coming to ask you questions about Elliot."

"Maybe they aren't coming here," Anne said. The phone rang.

"Hello, Amy! Oh, thank you . . . they are? Thank you! Thank you!" Anne said.

"Gladys! That was Amy! The TV news reporter is on his way here! Amy said she was in her yard, and the driver stopped and asked her if he was in the right neighborhood for this street. I don't want to talk to them."

"You don't have to," Gladys said. "I'll answer the door and tell them you're not giving interviews. Is that all right with you?"

"That's fine."

They heard a car pull up in front of the house. They both looked out the living room window and saw a young man with a TV camera and another guy with a notepad getting out of a van.

"Go into the sunroom. I'll get rid of them."

Anne was on her way to the sunroom when the doorbell rang. She could hear some of the conversation from there. The reporter was rather pushy, saying he needed a statement from Elliot Winter's mother about whether she thinks her son is alive or dead. She heard Gladys tell him his mother wasn't giving any interviews. The reporter was insisting to see Elliot's mother, and Gladys was just as insistent. Finally, the reporter and his sidekick left.

"Anne!" called Gladys, as she came back to the sunroom. "I don't think they have really gone even though I saw them go up the street and turn at the corner. That guy was very pushy."

"I heard him," said Anne.

"I don't think you should stay here. They may be back when they see my car gone. Why don't you pack an overnight case and stay with me for a few days?"

"I hadn't planned on leaving here. But you're right. They might be back. And I don't want to talk to them. Well, I've watered all the flowers. They won't need any watering for several days. I'll take the mail with me and work on it at your place. And my cross-stitch."

Anne had all of her stuff packed in about thirty minutes. Gladys helped her carry her bags to the car. Anne made sure all the doors and windows were locked, as Gladys pulled down the garage door so no one would see the car from the street. They got into Gladys's car and made their getaway. A few minutes later, the TV news van pulled into Anne's driveway. The reporter spent about fifteen minutes ringing the doorbell and knocking on the door. His knocking was loud, so loud the immediate neighbors could hear him. The husband of the retired couple across the street walked over and told the reporter to quit making so much noise: Mrs. Winter had left with her friend.

"Do you know which way they went?" asked the reporter.

"No. I just saw them back out of the driveway and head towards town."

"Hell! I've got a three o'clock deadline. Come on," he said to the cameraman, "let's see if we can catch up with them."

They both jumped into the van. The reporter backed out of the driveway and sped down the street toward town.

The neighbor smiled. *Good thing I saw the gals turn left at the next street.* He laughed aloud.

Chapter 37

It was dark. Elliot could feel the dampness. As he slowly awakened, he heard the sound of water lapping gently against the earth. Or maybe it was lapping against the walls of a building. His eyes were adjusting to the darkness. What felt like a thin blanket covered him. He could see a vertical sliver of light, not far in front of him. Maybe it was a crack between a door and a wall. He smelled the decaying odor he associated with salt water. He smelled musty old papers, kerosene, and maybe old leather—or was it wood? He moved, and pain shot through his upper body. Something heavy was on his left arm and his right leg. He couldn't move. Where was he, and how did he get here?

The last thing he remembered was a sting to his chest and falling. There was something else too. What was it? He wondered how long he had been here. Someone had found him, he concluded, and put him here. Maybe whoever it was will make an appearance soon. *It's best not to panic*, he thought. He felt for his arm. A hard substance surrounded it. It must be a cast. *Broke my arm in the fall. I guess my leg, too, since it feels weighted down.* Whoever found him knew something about making casts, he reasoned. He wondered why he was here instead of in a hospital. Why did they hide him away in this dark place? He felt they would be back to check on him. He hoped it would be soon.

Chapter 38

Sarah and Jason were bombarded with requests for radio and TV interviews, which they declined through Mr. Abbot. Several weeks after Elliot's disappearance, they finally released a statement through their attorney that they hoped Elliot would be found alive. As to questions about the corporation, business would continue as usual.

Reporters camped out at the Edmondses' row house in Salem. With the help of some friends, Jennifer and Bob, Sarah and Jason slipped out of their row house several evenings later and took up residence in one of Jennifer and Bob's rental homes in Walden.

Jennifer and Bob dressed in clothes Sarah and Jason were previously seen in by members of the press gathered outside their home. Jennifer donned a wig that made her look like Sarah from a distance while Jason wore Bob's baggy trousers and golf hat. While Jennifer sat close to the bay window in the living room—but not too close to attract the reporters—Sarah and Jason with Ginger slipped out the back door. They left in Jennifer and Bob's dark green BMW sedan parked in the back, holding their breath that those waiting outside in front of their home wouldn't pay any attention to the car. They all knew the charade would be discovered eventually, but they hoped it would last long enough for Sarah and Jason to get to their temporary home. It worked. The reporters, four of them, were busy looking for something to stand on to look into the Edmondses' living room, while Sarah and Jason left almost unnoticed.

Jayne and Jim Wilson watched from their home across the street with a smile on their faces as the dark green BMW slipped down the lane and turned onto Essex Street. They had a feeling their neighbors, Sarah and Jason, were in the BMW. They decided not to go to church for bingo that evening. They were going to see how long it would take the reporters to discover that their "news" had escaped.

The next morning, while Jayne was putting breakfast on the table, she heard some yells from the front of the house. Jim called her to come and look. She left the kitchen in a hurry to join Jim at the living room window. One of the reporters yelled at the Edmondses' row house. He demanded they come out and answer some questions he and his fellow reporters wanted answers to.

"What brought this on?" asked Jayne.

Jim replied, "One of the reporters noticed the window shades in the bedroom used by Sarah and Jason hadn't been closed. I heard several of them wondering if they were in one of the rooms at the back of the house. Then a woman appeared in the living room window who looked a lot like Sarah. But it wasn't her. So, honey, we were right. Sarah and Jason were in the car that left from over there last night."

"I wonder if the reporters realize it isn't Sarah?"

"I don't know. Maybe they do and that is why they want them to come out."

"This is better than winning triple bingo," Jayne commented.

At that instant, one of the reporters, a large built, broad-shouldered man taller than the others, pounded on the Edmondses' front door. His long hair swept back in a ponytail, black leather jacket and earring in his left ear set him apart from the rest of the reporters. A male voice from an upper story window shouted, "Please go away. You're waking the neighbors with your noise." The reporter wasn't taking no for an answer. "It's your responsibility to the press to answer our questions," the reporter bellowed.

"Call and make an appointment with us. We'll answer your questions but not right now."

"Why not? Tell us if your wife was the one leaving Monrose after the shooting."

"Leave or we'll call the police."

As the reporter made demands, the Wilsons spotted a police car approaching in silence from one end of the lane. Flashing lights were at the other end. Several policemen climbed out of each car and rushed to surround the reporters.

"Let's quiet down," said one of the policemen, as he addressed the reporter at the door. "You're causing too much noise at this hour of the morning. The family inside called us and said you're harassing them. You leave now, or we take you to jail."

Several of the reporters mumbled to each other as they turned and ambled away. The ponytailed reporter didn't move from the front steps. "I want to talk to the couple who lives here," he told the policeman who addressed him.

"Apparently, they don't want to talk to you. It would be best if you leave and call them later in the day. Make an appointment with them."

"No way. I want to see them now. I want to know if Mrs. Edmonds is the woman who was seen leaving the mansion shortly after the shooting."

"In that case," said the policeman, "you're going to be a guest of the city." He climbed the steps toward the reporter to take him by the arm when the reporter leaped over the railing and ran. Two other policemen headed him off and caught him before he got to the end of the lane. One of the policemen handcuffed him, as the other read him his rights.

"What an exciting morning!" Jayne exclaimed.

"It sure is." They waited until the police left before returning to the kitchen.

"My breakfast is cold. Is yours?" Jim asked.

"Yes. No problem though. I'll put our plates in the microwave."

"We'll certainly have something to tell the gang at bingo tonight," Jim said with a smile.

Shortly after the police left, and while Jayne and Jim ate breakfast, Jennifer and Bob left the Edmondses' row house by the back door on foot. They went around to the front and looked up and down the lane. Seeing no one around, they headed toward Essex Street to their home.

Chapter 39

When Elliot awoke, he was startled by a presence next to him.

"Glad to see you awake. I thought you might not make it. I'm Rich. I pulled you out of the harbor. You're probably wondering who doctored you. I did. You see, I'm a registered nurse at Boston Hospital. I was a medic in Vietnam and learned how to patch guys up. You're in good hands with me."

Elliot couldn't see Rich too well in the dim light. His voice was friendly.

"What am I doing here? Why am I not in a hospital?" Elliot inquired, his voice hoarse from not talking.

"You came conscious for a few minutes after I fished you out of the water. You asked me not to take you to a hospital. You mumbled something about you didn't want someone to find you. I noticed a big yacht setting off the shore. Looked like whoever was on it was watching everything. I wondered why they didn't come to your rescue. The tide was washing you toward the yacht, then you got caught in a current that brought you toward me. I thought you might be in trouble, so I brought you here. I'm not sure if I did the right thing, though. Your mug was plastered all over the eleven o'clock news last night."

"Tell me, tell me what they said." Elliot cleared his throat to get rid of the hoarseness.

Rich told him that the newscasts said he was missing and presumed drowned. The reporters reiterated his life story and predicted that his body will be found soon. Divers were looking close to where he went over the cliff.

Elliot was wondering if he should ask Rich to take him to the hospital and let everyone know he was all right. But whoever shot him would know he was alive if he did that. Elliot thought he should wait until he was feeling a little better and see how the media would handle this. He wondered if they would find out what happened. Would they find out he swindled some of the company's funds? *Yes,* he thought, *it would be better to wait.*

"Thanks for helping me. How bad is the damage?" Elliot's voice was a little stronger.

"You were shot close to the heart. Another two inches to the right, and you would've been dead. Evidently, when you hit the water below, the bone in your right leg and your left arm were broken, along with some ribs on the left side."

"How long is it going to take me to heal?"

"At least a month."

"Am I going to have to stay here then?"

"No," replied Rich. "I'm going to move you in a few days. I'm getting a place ready for you right now. I had a feeling you'd pull through. We'll have to be quiet about it, though. I wouldn't be surprised that the guy on the yacht may be waiting for news of your demise. He probably won't be satisfied until your body is found. I got you some soup here. Want to try some?"

"Sure."

Rich added another pillow under Elliot's head and gave him several spoonfuls.

"This is good," Elliot said. He took a few more spoonfuls.

"Where is this place?"

"You know those islands that you can see from Salem and from Beverly?"

"Yeah."

"We're on one of them."

"Why here?"

"It was the closest place to take you. Besides, my uncle owns this one. The family comes here for the family reunion. And we've already had it this year. This is one of the few islands that's not covered at high tide," Rich explained.

"That's good to know."

"I'm leaving you a battery-operated lantern and some newspapers. Thought you might want to read what's being said about you. This sack has a thermos of soup, crackers, and bottles of water. I'll be back in the morning to check on you. Stay still, move as little as possible. If you haven't noticed, you're on a bedpan." *Yuck*, thought Elliot.

A few minutes after Rich left, Elliot picked up the newspapers and scanned them.

"Well, well. Sarah now has the family fortune," he sneered. "And I'm presumed dead. Hell, you're not rid of me yet."